THE WORST SPIES IN THE SECTOR

Book Two of Dumb Luck
and Dead Heroes

Skyler Ramirez

Copyright © 2023 Skyler S. Ramirez

All rights reserved

The characters and events portrayed in this book are fictitious. Any similarity to real persons, living or dead, is coincidental and not intended by the author.

No part of this book may be reproduced, or stored in a retrieval system, or transmitted in any form or by any means, electronic, mechanical, photocopying, recording, or otherwise, without express written permission of the publisher.

ISBN-13: 9798864698747

Printed in the United States of America

To my bookworm daughter, who keeps saying she'll get to my books when she's done with the latest Rick Riordan series.

CONTENTS

Title Page
Copyright
Dedication
Foreword
Prologue — 1
Chapter 1 — 5
Chapter 2 — 11
Chapter 3 — 19
Chapter 4 — 26
Chapter 5 — 32
Chapter 6 — 37
Chapter 7 — 41
Chapter 8 — 49
Chapter 9 — 52
Chapter 10 — 55
Chapter 11 — 57
Chapter 12 — 65

Chapter 13	69
Chapter 14	75
Chapter 15	80
Chapter 16	90
Chapter 17	95
Chapter 18	99
Chapter 19	102
Chapter 20	109
Chapter 21	118
Chapter 22	126
Chapter 23	130
Chapter 24	137
Chapter 25	140
Chapter 26	144
Epilogue	148
Books By This Author	155
About The Author	159

FOREWORD

I love my readers. The outpouring of support I've gotten for the first book in this series, *The Worst Ship in the Fleet*, is just what any author dreams of. I've enjoyed reading all your comments and reviews, even the not-so-flattering ones. I *love* it when you reach out to me on social media and tell me how much you enjoy my books, and I try to respond to as many of you as I can. You're the reason I write.

If you haven't read the first book of this series yet, I highly recommend you do so before you read on, as there will be major spoilers ahead. And while each book in this series will have its own unique story and messy situation for our 'dead heroes' to overcome, they do all fit into the larger narrative of Brad Mendoza and Jessica Lin. If you want a quick way to get through Book One, I'm pleased to share that *The Worst Ship in the Fleet* audiobook will be released on Audible and iTunes any day now (late October 2023).

A lot of you have mentioned really wanting to see how our two heroes reacted to their 'deaths' in Book One. We delve into some of that in the chapters to come, though we're still experiencing it all from Brad's standpoint. So, we get his reactions, filtered through his own self-awareness (or supreme lack thereof at times). And we only get Jessica's thoughts and reactions insofar as Brad understands them. And let's be honest, Brad is kind of an idiot, especially when it comes to women.

Still, if you read between the lines, you'll learn a lot more about these two wonderful characters in this second book. And book three, which is coming in January 2024, will go even deeper into their pasts and reveal more of the secrets teased in Book One. After all, I can't reveal it all at once! How boring would that be?

As with all my books, there are no graphic scenes in this one, and there is no swearing. So, sit back, relax, and enjoy another chaotic ride with Brad and Jessica. And let me know what you think! (www.facebook.com/skylerramirezauthor and www.instagram.com/skyler.ramirez.author/)

Thanks,

Skyler Ramirez

PROLOGUE

"Brad, you're an idiot."

How come people always feel the need to tell me that? It's not as if I don't already know! As I've said many times before, my stupidity is an incontrovertible fact!

Yet nearly everyone in my life seems intent on reminding me of it at every opportunity. My ex-father-in-law, the illustrious windbag Admiral Terrence Oliphant, was always especially fond of explaining to me in very colorful ways how little he admired my intelligence. My ex-wife, Carla, toward the end, said it not with words but with her eyes. I know that sounds dramatic, like something out of a cheap romance novel. But Carla had a way of conveying entire *epic poems* with just her eyes. I used to love that about her until those poems turned into indictments against me.

Even my own mother, the day after my divorce was finalized, told me straight to my face just how dumb I was for driving my wife into the arms of another man. Gee, Mom, I'm pretty sure Carla had something to say about that choice. But listen to Paula Mendoza tell it, and I may as well have physically pushed Carla into bed with that dandy Horace Clarington, and somehow, in the process of falling, she lost her clothes along the way!

Yes, many people have called me dumb, stupid, idiot, and a host of more colorful synonyms in the last six months, but *none* of them hurt me as much as these four simple words do now.

Perhaps it's because the person who just called me an idiot is quite literally the *only* person in the galaxy I can now count on as a friend, partner, or even acquaintance! After all, everyone else, even my mother, thinks I died in the Gerson system three days ago.

So, I look up from where I'm sitting on my bunk on board our new ship, the *Wanderer*, at the lithe but somehow looming figure of Jessica Lin, who just finished giving that simple yet scathing opinion of me. I've known her now for a very long and eventful week, yet every time I see her, it still takes my breath away. She's shorter than me, about 175 centimeters, with straight black hair and other Asian facial features. And *everything* about her, from her face to the curve of her waist into her hips, is absolutely *perfect*. But she's mad at me right now, so she's...crying? Wait, why is she crying?

I was expecting Jessica to be glaring angrily at

me and the nearly empty bottle of scotch I just finished downing in a vain attempt to escape the reality of my death. But I'm surprised to find no anger in her expression. Instead, her stunning face is wet with tears that run in rivulets down her cheeks.

Now, any heterosexual man will tell you, at least if he's being honest, that few things can evoke emotion in a man more than the sight and sound of a woman crying. I know it sounds sexist, but it awakens some kind of primal instinct in us from way back in the day when we lived on only one planet, and men were expected to defend the honor of their women by throwing rocks at each other or slapping each other with little white gloves. Or something like that; I never listened in history class. If it didn't have anything to do with flying through the stars and shooting stuff with really big lasers, I was never all that interested.

But now, I get to feel a new and exciting emotion! One that I haven't allowed myself to feel in quite some time:

Shame.

I get unsteadily to my feet and look again at the bottle in my hand. There are a few last milliliters of scotch left sloshing around in the bottom, and they call to me with their sweet promise of oblivion and forgetfulness. I yearn to take them up on their offer.

But then I look back up at the tear-streaked face of Jessica Lin, and I reach out to her with the hand holding the bottle. She understands, taking it from me and putting it behind her back, where its siren song doesn't call out to me quite so strongly.

"OK," I say, trying extremely hard not to slur my words. "Let's go figure out what we're going to do now that we're dead."

CHAPTER 1

Things Cost Money

Do you know how much it costs to run a starship? I didn't.

When your entire adult life is spent in the Navy, trivialities like the cost of operating the ships you serve on don't often come up. When you need fuel, a tanker is there to provide it. When you need more missiles, a tender comes alongside, and you're good to go. When your uniform wears out, you get a new one from the quartermaster. When you need booze, you find whatever still the enlisted spacers have set up, and you 'confiscate' it and the product. And on and on and on.

Oh sure, I had my life outside of the Navy with Carla while we were still married. But she handled all the money, and we always seemed to have enough of it. I always suspected that good ole Terrible Terrence was giving her money on the side to augment my meager officer's salary. The Oliphants are kind of a big deal in Promethean society, and they have a lot of money from mysterious sources. They didn't always, but somehow Carla's dad went from rags to riches, all while on a government salary. Sketchy, I know.

OK, honestly, I *knew* that my father-in-law was giving us money on the side. I just never wanted to admit it, even to myself. There's an aspect of pride to being an adult where you really do want to provide for yourself and your spouse without accepting anyone else's charity. But I also knew when I married her that Carla had expensive tastes. She had *so* many shoes in her closet and still bought new ones all the time. So, she obviously took her daddy's money and didn't tell me, and I never asked. And we both lived more-or-less happily with the fiction of it all.

Until we didn't, but it wasn't money that drove us apart. It had more to do with me becoming a mass murderer. But I digress.

Anyway, what I really mean to say is that I'm realizing now that I more or less have no *clue* how the real universe works. I don't know how to pay bills or even what those entail for running a starship. And the thought of learning about that stuff gives me a headache…or maybe that's still the hangover from yesterday or the day before. They all blend together sometimes.

Either way, I'm not about to go build some

spreadsheets or something boring like that to figure out just how broke Lin and I are. Because running a starship is *expensive*. I know enough to be daunted by that. There's fuel, water, foodstuffs, thruster reaction mass, toothpaste, soap, and booze. We can't forget the booze. Agent of the King's Cross Heather Kilgore, when she let us steal *Wanderer* from Gerson Station—I suspect it was a ship set aside for her personal use while there —was kind enough to leave a few bottles of the good stuff in the galley. But what I haven't already drunk, Lin has dumped down the sink.

But booze or not, we need *money*! Otherwise, our new lives as Ben Lopez and Jennifer Kim are going to be short and impoverished. By the way, I hate the new name Kilgore chose for me; my high school bully was named Ben.

It's only been a day since Jessica took my last bit of scotch, but all this thinking about money reminds me why I hate being sober.

"All I'm saying, *Captain*," Lin says to me now in the small ship's galley, breaking me out of my thoughts, "is that the only way this is going to work is if you take charge and *be* the captain."

I regard her across the table and the steaming plate of dehydrated potatoes that desperately make me miss Warrant Officer Hoag's cooking from *Persephone*. I honestly never thought I'd miss *anything* from that ship.

"Well," I respond, spearing another soggy potato with my fork and pointing it at her for emphasis, "the thing is, I'm not a captain anymore. And you're not a lieutenant commander anymore, Jessica. We're no longer in the Navy, so we don't have to think in those terms now. We can be anything we want. Like clowns."

She looks at me incredulously. Which, of course, means I need to explain myself. I feel like I have to do a lot of that with her.

"No, seriously. I went to the circus once with my mom when I was a kid. I saw like fifteen clowns get out of a tiny rocket, and I thought to myself, wouldn't it be so cool to be a clown and travel the galaxy in a tiny little starship with fourteen of my closest friends? For something like two years, all I wanted to be was a clown until someone told me that the Navy would let me shoot things. Clowns don't get to shoot stuff."

She's still frowning, trying to decide if I'm being serious—which I am—or mocking her—which I also am. So, I do what most guys do when they've put their foot in their mouth with a pretty girl: I double down.

"Come on, Jessica. Didn't you ever want to be anything other than a naval officer? Or did you come home from the hospital saluting your parents and spouting naval regulations?"

She shakes her head. "I don't know. I can't remember back that far."

Ugh. If she's going to insist on having no sense of humor, this new life will end up being *really* long for both of us. Actually, never mind, because we'll die first from starvation when we run out of food and have no money to buy more. But we'll be bored the entire time we're starving.

"Listen, Brad," she says my name for the first time since she called me an idiot yesterday. It sounds foreign coming off her tongue as if she's totally out of place calling anyone anything other than 'sir, yes sir, right away sir!'.

"I don't remember what I wanted to be as a kid," she continues, "but I know what I am now. And even though I've been…ripped out of the Navy, I'm still a naval officer at heart. And so are you. And if we don't stick with what we know, then…"

She trails off, and I can see her eyes starting to water up. And I don't particularly want to feel like a horrible human being for making her cry a second day in a row. Even mass murderers have to draw the line somewhere. So, I decide that surrender is the better part of valor.

"Fine. I'm the captain again. Happy? But you can't

be the XO, not on a civilian ship. People will get suspicious. So, you're my first mate. Got it?"

She nods, a look of relief on her face that tells me that she genuinely is grasping for a lifeline with this whole 'act like we're still in the Navy' thing. Maybe being dead is easier for me; after all, my naval career all but ended six months ago. And with Carla, I at least had a life outside the Navy for a little while. But, as far as I can tell, Lin hasn't known *anything* outside the Promethean Navy for her entire adult life. So perhaps I just need to give her this.

"Got it," she finally responds.

"Good," I say, and then I have a wicked thought. "And as my first order to my new first mate, I need you to go and figure out what it's going to cost to run this ship and keep food in the galley. Report back to me at 0800 tomorrow with your findings. Scratch that; make it 1100. I want to sleep in."

She frowns.

"Fine," I say begrudgingly. "Oh nine-thirty, and not a moment sooner!"

I've never seen anyone so happy to be ordered to go and build a spreadsheet.

CHAPTER 2

*Picking a New Career
(Lin Ruins Everything)*

"Three weeks? Really? That's all we have?" I try and fail to keep the frustration out of my voice. I haven't had a drink in two full days now, and going that long without has me seriously on edge. Not to mention, I slept terribly last night, knowing that the first thing I got to do upon waking was review a depressing spreadsheet. And I wasn't disappointed!

"That's what the numbers say," Jessica says hesitantly. "I can recheck them; maybe I made a mistake somewhere."

"No, no, no," I say, waving her down as she starts to get up from the small table in *Wanderer's* galley. "I'm sure your math is fine. I'm just not used to having to worry about where my next meal is coming from. It kinda…"

"Sucks?" she finishes for me with a timid shrug. "At least we have three weeks if we keep our jumps to a minimum and don't eat huge meals. I'm sorry."

I don't know why she's apologizing, but it's not a good sign. I badly need 'Confident Lin' right now, the woman who devised the plan to destroy a heavily armed Scimitar-class destroyer using the barely-spaceworthy *Persephone*. What I *don't* need is for her to go back to doubting herself. Because at least one of us needs to be intelligent and decisive, and it sure isn't going to be me.

"It's not your fault, first mate," I say in my best imitation of my old command voice. "It's just the reality of the situation. So, what do we do about it?"

She sits up straighter. I'm quickly learning that Confident Lin usually emerges when she sets her brilliant mind to solving a problem. It's why I asked her to take on the task of figuring out our finances; well, that and because it was a great way to pay her back for forcing me to keep pretending I'm a captain. But either way, Lin needs problems to solve as much as I need alcohol to drink.

"We have to stop thinking like we're still in the Navy," she says slowly, directly contradicting what she told me yesterday. I'm smart enough not to call her out on it.

She continues, "And that means we have to figure out what skills we have and how to monetize them, and quickly."

"I can play chopsticks on the piano," I say with a half-smile, trying to lighten the mood. She throws me an irritated frown like my mother did when she caught me trying to light the drapes on fire when I was eight. It turns out Confident Lin also comes out when she's annoyed with me. Great, that should be easy to maintain.

"I can drive and fight a ship," she says through her frown, "but I don't know much about keeping it running."

"Neither do I," I admit. "At least, beyond the basic engineering courses from the Academy, but you and I both went the tactics and command track, so they didn't exactly spend much time teaching us to maintain a reactor."

She nods. "But we *can* drive the ship. And probably better than most merchant pilots out there."

"Might make us good smugglers," I say, only half joking.

Lin frowns again. "No, we need to try and stay on the right side of the law; avoid attention." It's a naïve statement, considering we're in a stolen ship with fake identity papers, but I get where she's coming from. Neither one of us has the makings of a criminal mastermind.

"OK, what do you suggest then?" I need to keep her working the problem and not focusing on what we *can't* do. I don't think either of us is coping well with our sudden and unexpected deaths five days ago at Gerson, but this is the most animated I've seen her since then.

She thinks for a long moment, and I let the silence go on while I watch her mind work. Finally, she nods. "Maybe not smugglers, but we *can* be merchant spacers. This ship has a good-sized cargo hold for its tonnage. If we can haul high-margin goods, it should cover our living and operating expenses and then some."

Wanderer—it's not the ship's real name, but it's the one we've decided to use—looks about like what you would expect for a smallish merchant freighter. It's essentially two large boxes laid end-to-end for a total length of about fifty meters and an overall width of around ten. The forward box is the cargo hold. The aft box contains the main drive, with exhaust nozzles coming out the stern. It also holds the reactor and the jump drive, the latter of which is a rarity for a ship this size. On top of both boxes and running the length of the ship is the crew area, where we are now, narrower than the boxes and shaped like a flattened cigar with tapered ends.

In other words, our ship looks like a very pregnant whale. But be it ever so humble, she's home.

And Lin's right; the box that makes up our cargo hold is large for a ship this size. I've stopped enough smugglers in my day to have plenty of reference points for comparison.

So, we should be able to make a living, I suppose, by hauling cargo. It just sounds so...*boring*. While I know I should be grateful to be alive after all that happened in Gerson, like Lin, I'm facing the harsh realization that my old life as a Navy captain is over, and my new life as a civilian is off to a terrible start. Besides, the life of a cargo hauler is one of the last I would have ever chosen for myself. They don't even get to shoot stuff!

"What about hiring out as mercenaries?" I suggest hopefully. When I was a teenager, my favorite series of books was about a daring mercenary outfit who managed to save an entire star system from pirates and were paid enough to literally *buy* their own small planet. Then their leader, the dashing Billy Firebrand, managed to parlay that into building a more extensive fleet, hiring more troops, saving a princess, marrying said princess, and eventually being named the monarch of a coalition of systems that could rival anything in the Inner Rim worlds. All while he fought for truth, justice, beautiful women, and lots of money.

It was a ridiculous story, but that didn't stop fourteen-year-old me from absolutely idolizing Billy Firebrand and wanting for all the universe to grow up to *be* him. And besides disappointing my father, those stories were a big part of why I joined the Promethean Navy.

But from the expression on Lin's face, she must have missed reading the *Adventures of Firebrand's Marauders*. Too bad; she'd make a great Princess Nikita Starshine.

"We have a few extra cabins," she says, not even entertaining my fantastic mercenary idea. I'll have to suggest it again later and see if I can wear her down. "We could haul passengers along with cargo."

I nod and don't express my deep disappointment at not being the next Billy Firebrand. "That could work. And aside from food and water costs, it would be pure margin on top of the cargo. I think it's a great idea." What I'm actually thinking is, 'Stupid Lin and her stupid non-Billy Firebrand practicality'. But even I realize I'm being petulant, so I keep those thoughts to myself.

Then she lights up at my compliment, and all thoughts of playing mercenary flee my head. Lin is stunning at her worst. In those rare moments when she's happy about something, she's absolutely breathtaking. Enough to make me forget all about Billy Firebrand, Nikita Starshine, Scooter James, and the rest of the Marauders.

"OK," she says as if it's all settled, "but the next question is where do we go to get a cargo?"

I consider her query and order my implant to bring up a map of nearby star systems in share mode so Lin can see it, too. I scan the names of the closest systems, not recognizing most of them, until one jumps out at me.

"Kate's Hope," I say.

She nods in agreement. "Independent system, known for a pretty laissez-faire government, and a shipping hub for this sector. Intelligent choice."

I nod as if I were thinking all the same things and not as if I simply picked Kate's Hope because it sounded...well, hopeful. I'm not familiar with this part of space; few people know much of what's outside their home *system,* and far fewer know of what's outside their entire star *nation.* In the Promethean Navy, we mainly studied star nations, systems, and planets we might have to fight, and nothing out this direction was ever on that list. But Lin often shows surprising depths of knowledge, and I can see why she was such a fast-rising star in the Navy before whatever happened to her on the destroyer *Ordney* ended all that.

"All right, first mate," I tell her. "Set a course for Kate's Hope and jump the ship. I'm going down to engineering to see if I can make any sense of things in case we have a problem."

She gets up briskly and leaves the tiny galley to head toward the bridge—really more of a cockpit—of our small ship. And, alone finally, I start rummaging through the galley cupboards to see if that bottle of scotch from two days ago has a brother somewhere that Lin hasn't managed to find and throw out.

If this were a story in *The Adventures of Firebrand's Marauders*, I, the hero, would have sworn off alcohol after the events on *Persephone*. I would be a fully redeemed and changed man. But, as Lin just painfully drove home, this isn't a Billy Firebrand story. And while I do feel much better about myself than I did a week ago, when I first arrived at Gerson and met Jessica, none of that has rid me of the cravings. Frankly, I'm not even sure I *want* to stop drinking. Reality is just terrible these days.

CHAPTER 3

Hope Dashed

"What do you mean we can't take your cargo?" I ask in what I have to admit is a much more frustrated than professional tone. But the guy sitting at the big desk in the tiny office off Hope Station's main concourse deserves it.

"Listen," I continue, jabbing a finger in the air toward his chest. "You have stuff, and you need to get that stuff from here to the Mondez system, right?" I don't wait for him to respond, but now I jab the thumb of that same hand into my own chest. "I have a ship, and that ship can take your stuff to Mondez, for which you can give me money. You get your cargo to Mondez; I get paid. Everyone wins. So, what's the problem?"

The shipping broker holds out his hands and shrugs, though I can tell he's annoyed that I've been speaking to him like he's a particularly dull kindergartner. "Like I told you, Captain…Lopez, was it? You haven't been able to provide me with a cargo hauler's bond or even a ship's registration. Without those, no one will trust you to haul their cargo, and you're lucky if the local constables haven't already impounded your ship over lack of ownership papers. We respect the law here, you know."

It's already been a long and frustrating day. Still, I'm not proud to say that this is where I start yelling at the guy, using some language that no proper stuffy Promethean Naval officer would ever admit to having in his vocabulary. However, I've heard my ex-father-in-law yelling at the screen during football games, so I know better. I also recently learned some new words from a really annoying but very creative ensign on *Persephone*. I try out some of those now.

Luckily, Lin grabs me by the arm and drags me out of the tiny office before I can get too deep into questioning the broker's parentage and implying some pretty terrible things about his mother. My own mother would have slapped me, but I was just getting started. Ensign Stevens would be proud.

I'm about to shake Lin off and turn around to head back into the office and deliver a devastating zinger I just thought of about the hairy mole on the guy's chin, but my first mate's grip tightens around my arm, and I look to find her staring not at me, but at something across the concourse. I turn and follow her gaze, the mole-chinned broker forgotten for the moment.

The main concourse is the largest open area of the station, and it's pretty crowded this close to the local lunch hour. But I have no trouble picking out the guy Lin is focused on, mostly because he's the only person in the place staring openly back at me. Then he starts walking toward us, his eyes riveted on mine.

My first thought is that he's a member of the constabulary that the broker we just left not-so-subtly threatened to call on us. But nothing about him screams 'cop'; not that I've had a whole lot of interaction with the police outside of Navy cops and MPs, and they're easy to spot from a kilometer away. They walk funny because they have sticks surgically implanted…well, you know.

But still, I don't think this guy's a cop because about halfway to me, he breaks eye contact and looks around furtively as if he's *also* worried about the constables. So, I decide to stay put and let him come to us. This could be interesting.

Lin doesn't think so. I can tell she's itching to run. So now I have a moral imperative to stand my ground and show her I'm not afraid. After all, as she likes to point out, I'm the *captain*.

The guy stops just a meter away from us, his eyes still on mine, though they quickly flash to Lin so he can give her a quick once over. Who wouldn't? But she's totally out of his league; I mean, the guy is shorter than she is, and he looks like his nose has been broken and poorly reset more than once. He's also bald, but not in the cool way some big muscular actors are bald; more like an accountant who wears a funny straw hat so the top of his hairless head doesn't burn in the sun.

I'm picturing the guy now in a straw hat holding a calculator when he finally speaks. "Excuse me, might you be the owners of that ship docked at airlock B32?" He speaks in a lazy, almost disinterested tone at odds with the intense way he's looking at me.

"Depends on who's asking," I respond, trying to match my tone to his like I'm already bored with the conversation.

"Owen Thompson," he says, reaching out a hand toward me and taking a small step forward.

Throwing caution to the wind, I reach out and clasp his hand with my own. If he's a cop, this would be when he uses the handshake to pull me closer and slap cuffs on my wrist. But he doesn't do that. Instead, his cold, dry hand gives mine a quick shake and then releases it.

His eyes dart around again, maybe still checking for constables. "I hear that your ship is available for hire. Cargo and passengers."

It sounds like it should be a question, but he doesn't phrase it like one.

"You hear a lot for someone we've never met," I say skeptically. Next to me, Lin stiffens at my tone; leave it to her to take offense on behalf of a random accountant who's clearly stalking us or something. But I was intentional with my statement and my tone. I want to see how this guy reacts when thrown off balance. It will help me learn more about him.

Not *everything* I do is stupid.

Owen Thompson, to his credit, takes it all in stride. Maybe he's not an accountant after all. "I make it my business to hear things," he says calmly. "And I may have an opportunity for you."

"Listen," Lin starts, "we're not interested in anything ill—"

"What my first mate means to say," I interrupt her—I'm so going to pay for that later, "is that we're pretty confident of finding a standard cargo to a nearby system. So, we're not looking for anything…special right now."

Owen Thompson doesn't visibly react. He's a cooler customer than he looks.

"Then we're in luck," he says, "I have a legitimate business proposition for you. I'm looking for passage for me and a few friends to Namora, and I wanted to inquire if I might hire you and your ship."

My first inclination is to tell him no. There's

something definitely off about the guy. But then I remember just how much money we have—which is zero—versus how much we need—which is a lot—versus how many shipping brokers have already told us no today—which is also a lot.

"How many friends?" I ask.

"There are four of us. And a small bit of cargo."

I consider this. It is the best—well, the only—offer we've gotten today. I honestly don't know how we'll even pay the docking fees that this station extorts out of ships that stop here.

"And you said to Namora. Straight shot?" I quickly check my implant and see that the Namora system and its namesake planet are only two jumps away.

But he shakes his head. "No. Our cargo is in the Fiori system. We'll need to stop there on the way and pick it up."

Another quick check of the implant shows that Fiori is one of three inhabited systems that sit roughly between Kate's Hope and Namora, one jump away from each. But it's the furthest out of the three, so it's a stretch to call it 'on the way'."

Owen doesn't wait for me to argue. "What are your rates?" he asks as if I've already agreed to consider taking his business. Presumptuous of him, even if he is right.

Before we got off *Wanderer* and onto the station, I had Lin do more spreadsheet work and figure out what we need to charge to make any profit off various trips of different lengths. She loaded her dumb little spreadsheet onto my implant, so now I can look up the correct rate. But I've always been terrible with spreadsheets, and I'm struggling now to find the right number.

"Nine thousand credits," Lin says from beside me, and I barely stop a sigh of frustration. Even without her cells full of numbers and equations, I know that's *way* more than we need to charge for such a short hop. She obviously doesn't want him to…

"Agreed," Owen says without pause, sending more alarm bells through my head. Definitely not an accountant. An accountant would know better than to accept a deal like that. I'm about to open my mouth and argue, but he keeps talking. "My friends and I will be at your docking bay in an hour. I trust you'll be ready to go then."

Without waiting for a response to his sort-of question, he turns and walks away, just like that! Not even a backward glance. Leaving me and Lin to stare dumbly at each other.

CHAPTER 4

The Giant I Want to Punch

True to his word, Owen shows up precisely an hour later at *Wanderer's* airlock, three others with him, each carrying a small duffel bag and nothing more. He steps forward and rings the airlock chime while his three 'friends' hang back in the corridor.

I study the three I haven't seen before through the external camera before I open the hatch. Two are men, and one of those is quite possibly the biggest guy I've ever seen in person. He makes my old nemesis, Petty Officer Nedrin Jacobs, back on *Persephone*, look puny by comparison. He's tall, muscular, and pasty white with a flat, red-mottled face. I take an instant dislike to the guy. The other man is about my height and of average build, with dark skin and hair, and he looks like he might have some Indian ancestry. He's dressed sloppily, and his hair is a mess. I don't hate him quite as much as the big guy.

The third and final of Thompson's friends is a woman. She's shorter than Owen himself and has a feisty look about her, as if she's searching for an excuse for a fight. She's slim and trim with brown hair and olive skin. I like her, predictably, I suppose. I'm a sucker for a pretty face. When she turns to say something to the big guy, I catch her profile. She has a nice butt, though not nearly in the same league as Lin's.

I open the hatch and step out. "This everyone?" I ask with false joviality as I once again grasp Owen Thompson's hand. Same as before, it's slightly cold, but at least it's dry.

"This is Tucker," he motions toward the big guy first. "And that's Harris and Jules." Both men meet my eyes, but only Harris, the dark, sloppy one, gives a slight smile and nod. Tucker may as well be considering how I might taste for lunch. He probably needs a lot of calories every day.

The woman with the decent butt, Jules, just frowns when I meet her gaze as if she's evaluated me that quickly and has come away disappointed. That's good; it gets the awkwardness out of the way. I eventually disappoint *everyone*, so it's better if they know it's coming up front.

Lin isn't happy that we're taking this job, though even she had to begrudgingly admit that we really have no other options. But she's still mad at me and decides at this moment to ignore my order to stay on the ship while I negotiate the final particulars. I hear her step through the airlock hatch behind me, and the eyes of all three of Owen's friends flash to her. The big guy, Tucker, grins in a way I especially don't like.

"Well," I say to draw their attention back to me. "If you're ready to go, let me show you to your rooms. We only have three open bunk rooms, so two of you will need to share."

I'm half hoping that this revelation will make them reconsider hiring us; as much as we need the money, nothing feels right about this. But no such luck. They all seem to take it in stride.

Owen picks up the small duffel from the ground at his side and starts to walk past me through the outer hatch, but I put a hand on his chest to gently but firmly stop him in his tracks. I pretend not to notice Tucker bristle at this. Owen, for his part, shows no reaction but looks at me calmly. That lack of expected emotion sends a weird chill down my spine.

"There's, uh, the matter of payment," I say uncertainly. This is literally the first time in my life I've had to negotiate a business deal, and I'm not even sure what the protocols are.

"Of course," the probably-not-an-accountant responds as if he were expecting the question. "Half now; half when we arrive with our cargo on Namora."

I nod, though I don't know enough to decide if that's a good deal. My implant pings me then that it's been offered a connection from Owen's. I accept and watch 4,500 credits magically appear in the new blockchain account Lin set up as soon as we got in range of the planetary internet earlier today. I fight not to show my relief that we are no longer destitute.

"Do you need to fuel up before we go?" Owen asks.

I shake my head. "We've got plenty. Foodstuffs too. We can be underway as soon as you're all on board."

He looks down at my hand still on his chest meaningfully, and I lower it sheepishly. I've faced down self-proclaimed pirate *admirals* and even actual admirals in the Promethean Navy, but being here now, out of my element, has me feeling like a new midshipman all over again. I'm unsure of even what to do with my hands now, so I hook them on my belt.

"You gonna show me to my bunk, sweetheart?" Tucker speaks for the first time, leering at Lin's chest.

I instantly feel a wave of anger, and I remove my hands from my belt and ball them into fists. I'm opening my mouth to call the whole thing off when Owen beats me to the punch.

"Tucker!" he snaps in something akin to my old Navy command voice. It's the first time I've seen him show emotion, and it startles me. "That is an unacceptable way to speak to our hosts. Apologize, now!"

Owen may be a petite accountant-type, and Tucker three times his size, but the big man instantly looks cowed. Staring down at his hands and refusing to meet Owen's gaze, he mumbles an apology in Lin's general direction.

I turn my gaze to Owen and see a frown on his face. But he gives a curt nod, then turns and resumes walking through the open airlock. Looking back at Tucker, I see him glaring at me, hatred almost brimming over in his eyes and the hard set of his mouth. But he breaks eye contact first, picks up his bag, and follows his boss—because what I just saw makes it abundantly clear Owen *is* the boss here and not just some 'friend'—into the open airlock.

Behind him goes the woman, Jules, without even glancing my way. I still watch her butt for a second or two as she passes. It's growing on me. That leaves only Harris, the one who smiled at me earlier. But he's not smiling now; instead, he's watching Tucker's retreating back with an expression of concern. Then he looks at me and Lin. "Watch yourselves," he says in a low voice. "That one..." he nods toward where Tucker has now disappeared into our ship, "Well, don't let yourselves get caught alone with him."

Before either Lin or I can ask any clarifying

questions, he hurries off after his compatriots. I share a look with my first mate and shrug. She frowns, and I can see she's shaken, but she only nods in reply. I think we both have the distinct and unsettling feeling that the time when we could have backed out of this deal passed us stealthily at some point, and now we're in whether we want it or not.

But at least we have one thing going for us. Unless Owen is somehow magically familiar with all members of the Promethean Navy on sight, he can have no idea who he's dealing with.

Of course, that goes both ways. We have no idea who or what we're dealing with, either. For sure, it's not a group of traveling accountants.

CHAPTER 5

An Unappreciated Prank

It doesn't take much cajoling, not after the way Tucker acted toward her, to convince Lin to go to the cockpit while I show our new passengers to their cabins. I decide to take Harris' advice to heart, so I show him and Tucker to their shared room first, with Jules and Owen in tow.

Each of our crew cabins has a bunk bed, so I could have theoretically chosen any of the three to put the two men in. But I chose this one because it's the furthest from mine and Lin's cabins. There is also another…bonus to this room.

"Hey," Tucker complains loudly as he surveys the small space. "How am I even supposed to fit in that bed?"

I try not to laugh but keep an innocent expression on my face as if I have no idea what he's talking about—as if I don't notice there's a floor-to-ceiling wardrobe closet right at the end of the bunk that will prevent a tall person from letting their feet hang off the end of either of the small beds. And Tucker is *tall*.

"Tucker, you'll be fine," Owen says in a lazy voice, but it's enough to shut the big man up again. He angrily throws his duffel onto the lower bunk, glaring at Harris as if challenging the dark man to argue about being relegated to climb a ladder into bed.

Harris doesn't seem to mind, and from the small grin he throws my way, I can tell he's appreciating my unique sense of humor.

I take that opportunity to leave and show Owen and Jules to their rooms. We drop off Jules next. She doesn't even wait for me to show her the room's amenities but enters as soon as I key the door open and then shuts it behind her.

That leaves only Owen, and he frowns at me as we take the two steps down the corridor to his room. "You know," he says, his voice still casual, "you really shouldn't antagonize Tucker like that. He's actually not that bad of a guy. You just caught him in a sour mood. But I promise you there will be no trouble from him."

I try and look surprised, as if I have no idea what he's talking about. He shrugs like he doesn't care one way or the other.

Like Jules, he doesn't wait for me to show him the room. He bids goodbye at the door and then closes it behind him, leaving me in the corridor with my emotions hovering somewhere between glee at the thought of Tucker in the fetal position, trying to fit on the tiny bunk, and worry that maybe I've poked a bear once too many times. But mostly, I'm confused and worried by Owen. Something is unquestionably off about the guy, but I can't figure out what it is.

Lin is in the cockpit when I arrive, and she's even locked the door. I enter my captain's code to open it, and she turns at the sound, jumping a bit in her seat.

Now, I don't know everything that's happened to Lin in her past. I know she was a real up-and-comer in the Promethean Navy before *something* ended all that during her time as tactical officer on the destroyer *Ordney*. There was a point, while we were on *Persephone* and running from the enemy destroyer, where I thought she was about to share with me what had happened, but we were interrupted by the stupid ship's ion drive failing. Then, we were too busy saving our own lives and those of our crew to resume the conversation. Since then, I haven't found the right time to ask her.

What I *do* know is that she was being raped by her former captain *and* Petty Officer Nedrin Jacobs, the King's own nephew, for several months on *Persephone*. So, it's no surprise that a man like Tucker, who could be Jacob's larger cousin if it weren't for his gutter accent, would set her on edge. I mean, the guy puts *me* on edge, and I don't have nearly the emotional baggage that Lin has, at least not in that particular area.

"You OK?" I ask.

"I'm fine," she answers a bit too quickly. Nice try, but I used to be married. I know exactly what 'I'm fine' means. Or rather, I know exactly what it *doesn't* mean.

"I was thinking about ship security," I say as casually as I can. "I don't think we should give our new passengers access to the bridge. But, as captain, they will expect to have some access to *me*. So, my thought is that you should stay on the bridge as much as possible, with the door locked, and I'll tend to the passengers and their needs. Except when we're making a jump or docking or some such, then we should both be up here. Sound good?"

She regards me for several slow seconds, and I'm worried that she's going to argue and pierce the flimsy fiction I've set up around my reasons for the suggestion. But I'm relieved when she finally nods.

"Oh, and one more thing," I add as if it just occurred to me. "I don't think we should leave the bridge unattended, so I can bring you your meals here, and you and I can sleep in shifts." The implication is clear, despite my clumsy attempts to be nonchalant about it. This way, Lin will always be behind a locked door, either the one here in the cockpit—I keep calling it the 'bridge' out of habit, but it so isn't one—or the one on the hatch into her quarters. Safe and sound.

She nods again, with less hesitation this time, and I think I see a flash of gratitude in her green eyes. It turns out that, every once in a while, I can do something right.

I just hope she doesn't get used to that.

CHAPTER 6

*Underway and
Overwhelmed*

The next time I see our passengers is when I announce dinner through the intercom. I cooked. Yep. It's going to be horrible.

Not that Lin is any better of a cook than I am. Again, being Navy our entire lives, we didn't exactly make our own meals very often. And Carla and I ate out a lot, undoubtedly using her daddy's money. So, I haven't learned to do much other than rehydrate something using the auto-cook, which is exactly what I did for dinner tonight. By the way Lin wrinkled her nose when I took her plate into the cockpit, my rehydrated spaghetti turned out precisely how I expected it to.

Now, our four passengers file into the small galley and take seats around the even smaller table as I serve them their supposed meals. I'm half worried Owen will renege on the rest of our fee once he tastes the fare. But, surprisingly, none of them complain. Harris thanks me for the food. Jules grunts in my general direction. Most surprisingly, Tucker doesn't say anything at all, even though I literally handed him something to complain about on a plate!

They eat quickly and efficiently, not that there's any need to savor a meal like this. It may as well be Navy survival rations. Tucker asks, through a series of grunts and hand motions, for seconds, and I refill his plate. I don't even spit in it this time; I totally did on his first helping.

When they're all done eating and at some unspoken signal from Owen, the other three get up from the table and file past me back toward their cabins. A few seconds later, I hear a dull thud and the sound of a deep voice swearing, and I have to hold back a laugh. There isn't a ship in the galaxy designed for anyone as tall as Tucker, and his pain brings me a measure of joy.

Owen is still waiting there at the table, so I grab my own plate and sit across from my new and hopefully very temporary employer.

I have to say, my first bite of what I've cooked makes me marvel even more at Tucker's ability to keep his mouth shut all through dinner, and *especially* at his bravery to ask for seconds. It's terrible! I reevaluate my earlier thought: this is *worse* than Navy survival rations.

So, I'm half expecting Owen to complain about the food now that we're alone, but he watches me eat for a few moments and then broaches a different topic.

"How many hours to Fiori?"

I shrug and quickly check my implant. "We're still in Kate's Hope. Just under six hours more to the Fiori jump point and then another seven in transit. After that, depending on where your cargo is in the system, anywhere from four to forty hours to rendezvous and pick it up." I leave the implied question hanging in the air.

Luckily, he either takes the bait or was planning to tell me anyway. "It's at Fiori 2, on the Skytran Orbital."

I nod and consult my implant again. "So, about twelve hours from the jump point on the Fiori side. Do you mind me asking what the cargo is?"

He frowns, which is about the most severe facial expression I've seen him make since we met. "It's nothing too special," he responds. "Just some computer components we plan to sell in Namora. Pretty small crates that will fit easily in your hold. Is that going to be a problem?"

As if I have a choice at this point.

"No. No problem. As long as it's not dangerous and shows no signs of being dangerous," I almost add 'or illegal' but stop myself because I'm not sure I want to know.

"Good," Owen answers simply, then gets up and heads back to his room.

He leaves me behind with a bad feeling deep down in my gut. Because the chances that Owen is some sort of computer parts salesman are about as high as the chances of him being an accountant. There's something he's not telling me about his cargo, and I'm positive I'm not going to be happy when I find out what that is.

I look down at the remains of what is supposed to be spaghetti on my plate. I push the noodles around with my fork, but my appetite is suddenly gone. Then my implant alerts me that it's time for me to take my shift in the cockpit and let Lin get some sleep. So, I trash the remains of my plate, shove down my growing anxiety, and head to relieve my first mate.

CHAPTER 7

Story Time

The next morning, after a fitful half a night's sleep, I'm back in the cockpit with an equally sleep-deprived Lin. Seems neither one of us is doing well in that department these days. In fact, I can tell that she's a nervous wreck, but she seems to calm down the longer she's locked up here in the cockpit with me. Maybe I need to suggest that tonight she just sleep in the co-pilot's seat next to me while I take my shift, but I'm unsure of how to propose that without sounding overprotective.

We made the jump successfully at the end of my shift last night, and Lin took over most of the time in jump space before I joined her this morning. We'll emerge from our jump into the Fiori system in just a little while. She keeps asking me about the cargo, and I keep dodging the subject. No need for both of us to worry, though I can tell I'm not fooling her.

So, I decide instead to tell her about what I did to Tucker, putting him into the bunk that will make him contort like a pretzel to fit. To my surprise, she's more horrified than amused.

"Ben," we've agreed to use our new names this flight, even in private; no use risking a slip in front of our sketchy passengers, "why do you insist on antagonizing him like that? He already doesn't like us."

To my further surprise and hers, I bristle at the question. "And what should I do?" I ask. "Jess… Jen, if we don't stand up to bullies like that, they'll walk all over us. The best thing we can do with that giant is to keep him off balance. That way, he always has to ask himself what we know that he doesn't that gives us the confidence to spit in his eye." I don't tell her that I actually *did* spit in the man's spaghetti dinner.

She shakes her head, and I know that she's thinking. Or, at least, I think I do. She's thinking of Nedrin Jacobs and everything he did to her. I have no idea if she ever tried to stand up to the man or if whatever happened on the *Ordney* broke her so badly that she gave in without a fight. But I am sure that if she did try to stand up to him, it ended poorly for her. And Tucker, as I've mentioned, gives off major Jacobs vibes.

"Listen, Jen," I soften my tone. "They'll be off the ship in a couple of days, and their payment will give us enough profit to go and figure out how to get the registration and bonds that all those brokers were so worked up about at Kate's Hope. Then we can start hauling cargo on the up and up. You'll see. Things are going to turn out OK."

I can tell she's unconvinced, but my head hurts this morning. It's now been *four* days without alcohol for me; I didn't even have the cash to buy more on the station in Kate's Hope. So, instead of continuing to try to reassure her, I once again change the subject.

"Did I ever tell you about the time I took down an entire pirate flotilla on *Lancer*?"

It's such a weird segue that I can tell I caught her off guard, and she only shakes her head.

"We were on an extended patrol in the Corpus Christi cluster; you know how those go: running around and showing the flag. Battlecruisers like *Lancer* are good for that. Large enough to project power but a lot cheaper to operate than a battleship."

Of course, she knows all of this, but I say it anyway. It's my story, so I get to tell it how I want, and it's one I've told countless times at the stupid dinner parties Carla used to make me go to, so there's a rhythm to it. I lean back in the *Wanderer's* pilot seat, clasping my hands behind my head and staring at the stars outside the forward viewport with a little half grin on my face as if I don't have a care in the galaxy.

"Anyway, we're on our third stop, in a little Podunk system called Poe. You ever pass through there on a patrol?" I don't wait for her to answer. "Terrible little place. One station and only a few million people, mainly in the asteroid belt. It's a mining system with pretty much nothing else going on. The one inhabited planet is barely big enough to hold atmo. So, it all seemed like a pretty dull assignment, and I was more or less using it to rotate some of the junior officers through bridge duties and give them some hands-on training.

"Well, we're about two-thirds of the way through the system when we get a distress call from one of the nearby asteroid mining operations. Turns out a pirate flotilla, six ships ranging in size from heavy cruiser to destroyer analog, had exited jump space pretty close in and were burning full bore toward their little rock and broadcasting demands that they surrender or die. Somehow, the idiots hadn't seen us yet, or maybe they weren't looking.

"So, I had us cut acceleration and revector on thrusters so that our drive plume was hidden behind the bulk of our forward hull. Then we went full stealth mode, cutting off all EM and vectoring our drive nozzles to minimize our thermal signature. It helped that we could largely keep the asteroid between us and the pirate fleet for most of the trip in." I throw in the extra details I usually leave out at dinner parties because Lin will actually know what they mean. And I put my feet up on my console now, trying harder to look like a man who isn't being eaten inside by stress and ulcers. I doubt I'm fooling her, but she seems to be relaxing just slightly.

"They didn't see us until we were almost right on top of them, and by then, they had already turned over and were close to zero-zero intercept with the mining station. Well, we pop around the asteroid, and we're on them, and I mean within spitting distance. But even *Lancer* didn't have an even chance against all six of them."

As I always do, I pause there for dramatic effect and wait.

"So, what did you do?" Lin finally asks. She speaks! Victory!

I smile wider at her.

"Simple. I broadcast in the clear. Something to the effect of, 'All task force units attack on my mark; deadly force is authorized'. Now, they can only see *Lancer,* but the way we snuck up on them, I knew their leader had to be thinking about what *else* he might have missed out in the big dark. So, he doesn't waste any time but orders his ships to full burn back along their original course. And my tactical officer uses the big, bright thermals of their exhaust to put a trio of ship-killer missiles each right into the drive nozzles of their two largest cruisers."

I look over at her, grinning stupidly. I love this story. I heard they even made it a case study at the Academy, but that would have been after Lin graduated. And I can see just a hint of interest in her eyes, so it's working as intended. I keep going.

"Well, with their two biggest ships gone and their leader along with them, it took a few minutes for the remaining four ships to decide who had the authority to surrender on their behalf. But surrender they did. You should have seen the looks on their faces when they realized *Lancer* was all alone out there. But by that time, they'd shut down their reactors and couldn't put up a fight even if they'd wanted to. We disabled the rest, and our Marines barely encountered any resistance when they boarded each ship in turn."

I stop again and wait, watching her with that stupid grin still on my face. And slowly but inexorably, I see the corners of her mouth twitch up. Then she's smiling back at me, and I have to try hard not to shout for joy. And not just because Jessica Lin is the most beautiful woman I've ever seen, and double that when she's happy. But because I also know what a dark place she's been in since, and even well before, our deaths. So, at this point, I'll take even a single smile as a major win.

"Good story," she says without a hint of irony. "But not as good as the time my captain made me lead the Marine boarding party on Cantralla 7's orbital refinery to rescue hostages being held by the

Fringe Alliance terrorists."

"Oh, I've got to hear this," I tell her with genuine enthusiasm. And it turns out to be a great story, though not as good as my pirate one.

Still, it's opened the floodgates, and Lin is talking to me and laughing more than she has…well, ever. In fact, I'm reasonably certain that I've never once heard her laugh before now. I'd remember if I had; it's the most fantastic sound in the world. Like church bells on a Sunday afternoon mixed with the wind chimes at my grandpa's farm growing up. It reminds me of summer and puppies.

From there, we keep going with the stories well into the hours after we emerge from jump space into Fiori and pause only for a quick announcement on the intercom that we've arrived in-system. I tell her about the time I let a greased pig loose in Oliphant Hall at the Academy, and she tells me about putting itching powder all over the toilet seats in a men's dorm after one of the midshipmen there dumped her roommate for a first-year.

We talk and laugh until we're a third of the way toward our target station, when I finally decide, with great reluctance, that it's time for me to go make lunch for our passengers. I already let them fend for themselves regarding breakfast, and they're probably not too happy.

As I get up to leave, Lin surprises me by reaching

out to grab my wrist. Looking down, I see her smiling up at me. "Ben...Brad. Thanks," she says and then releases my hand. I nod and smile back, and then I have to almost drag myself the rest of the way to the hatch because now I *really* don't want to leave.

Outside in the corridor, I take a moment to lean against the nearest bulkhead and collect myself before making my way to the galley. And in that silent moment of solitude, I finally admit to myself something that has been building in the back of my mind since the day I first stepped foot on *Persephone*.

I'm in love with Jessica Lin. But there's no universe where she will ever love me back.

CHAPTER 8

The Other Shoe

Lunch is a largely silent affair, just like dinner last night. This time, the meal is simple sandwiches using some relatively fresh ingredients that Heather Kilgore or someone else left in the galley fridge when we took the ship. Even Tucker appears to enjoy the meal more, though I did manage to spit in his sandwich again.

"How much longer?" Harris asks, drawing an undecipherable look from Owen.

"We're just under eight hours out," I tell him, ignoring Owen altogether. "We'll turn over in another two hours to make our deceleration burn."

"Excuse me for just one moment," Jules says, getting up and leaving the galley. It's the most I've ever heard her say, and I watch her—or rather her butt—go but make no move to follow. Tucker and Owen strike me as the real threats, and I'm convinced now that Owen is the one I need to watch the closest.

He finally chooses to speak. "Will Miss Kim be joining us?" At least he hasn't learned Jessica's real name.

I shake my head. "I'm not comfortable leaving the cockpit unattended. Too many things can happen to a ship that a steady hand on the controls can react to far better than an AI."

He nods to acknowledge my response but says nothing more. I set about making a sandwich for myself and then join the three other men in eating silently.

Owen finishes the last bite of his sandwich and regards me again. "Ben, there's been a slight change of plans."

It takes a second for the words to register. My mind is elsewhere, on the beautiful hours I just spent swapping stories and laughing with Jessica. But when I finally recognize what he said, I cock my head in confusion. Then I see Tucker smile and Harris squirm in his seat.

Uh oh. I'm pretty sure the other shoe just dropped.

Owen doesn't wait for me to recover from my surprise. Instead, he keeps talking, though now more to himself than to me. "Let's see, right about now."

As if on cue, Jules reenters the galley, except now she's holding a pistol in one hand and the arm of a terrified Jessica Lin in the other.

"What's the meaning of this?!" I shout, but Owen ignores me, regarding Jules instead.

"Any problems?" he asks her.

She smiles and presses her gun deep into Jessica's ribcage, drawing a pained grunt from my first mate that almost has me leaping across the room to strangle the short woman, gun or no. "Not a one," Jules says. "The door lock was a simple hack, and I don't think the two of them even have any weapons on board. Fools."

"Owen, what is going on?" I demand again.

This time, he turns his cold eyes toward me. "As I said, Ben, there's been a change of plans. Or should I call you Captain Brad Mendoza?"

I already have my mouth open to shout another question at him, but hearing my real name uttered from his lips stops me cold. Then, my heart sinks even further as he turns his icy gaze to my first mate.

"And it's very nice to formally meet you as well, Lieutenant Commander Jessica Lin."

CHAPTER 9

*Mother Warned Me
About Days Like This*

If this were an *Adventures of Firebrand's Marauders* novel, the next thing that would happen would be Owen monologuing about his evil plan for twenty minutes, during which time Billy Firebrand would figure out his weakness along with those of all his cronies. Then, at the end of the monologue, Billy would say something clever and proceed to subdue and incapacitate each and every one of them...using only a toothpick.

But I'm not Billy Firebrand. I blame Lin for that. If she'd just said yes to us being mercenaries, we wouldn't be in this situation, and I'd be well on my way to emulating my boyhood hero.

But instead, I'm Brad Mendoza, the helpless idiot.

"Put her in her cabin," Owen says to Jules, and before I can object, the two women are gone. Now

I look back over to the three men still seated at my galley table, Tucker still contentedly munching on his second sandwich and reminding me of a particularly large pig my grandpa used to have on his farm.

"Owen, what is the meaning of this?" It's the third time I've asked a variation of the question and this time, he actually responds.

"Sorry, Captain Mendoza, but I find myself in need of your particular skillset, and I couldn't think of a better way to get your cooperation. Your first mate will be fine as long as you do *exactly* what I say." Tucker frowns at this in disappointment, but Owen ignores him.

"And just what exactly do you want from me?"

He takes in a deep breath and blows it out through pursed lips as if he's contemplating a rebuilding year for his favorite football team. "Well, you see, Brad—I can call you Brad, right?" I don't respond, so he takes it as a yes. "Brad, I need a Navy man for a particular job I've been hired to do. What's more, I need a senior naval officer who understands both the Prometheans and the Koratans. And, as you can imagine, there aren't too many of those just bumming around this sector of the Fringe."

"How do you know who we really are?" Wow! Maybe I should have, you know, denied being Brad Mendoza. Instead, I've just given him ironclad confirmation, just in case he had any doubts that maybe he's taken over the wrong ship crewed by two ex-Promethean Navy officers.

"That's not important," he says with a dismissive wave of one hand. "What's important is that you're going to help us with a little job here in Fiori. And if all goes well, you'll drop us off at Namora as planned and never see any of us again. You and your former XO can go your merry ways all safe and sound. But if things don't go well…" He pauses for dramatic effect, much as I did earlier telling my pirate story to Lin. "Well, let's just say that Tucker here would really like some alone time with Miss Lin."

Tucker grins widely at that comment, which lights a fire in me. So, I do something really foolhardy. I step across the room and land the most brutal punch I can right in the big man's face, smashing his sandwich in the process.

Before I even have the satisfaction of seeing him bleed—assuming I even hit him hard enough for that; his face felt like I was punching a steel bulkhead—I hear a whoosh and simultaneously feel a hard punch to my gut. I have just enough time to register the pistol in Harris' hand and the apologetic look on the dark man's face before several thousand volts of electricity from the stun round embedded in my stomach course through my body, and everything goes black.

CHAPTER 10

So Much For Bravery

I wake up slowly and painfully. It takes me a moment to figure out where I am, but I finally determine I'm on the hard metal deck of the Wanderer's galley, staring at the ceiling. Owen and his thugs just left me lying where I fell after the stun round hit me. So nice of them.

My other senses slowly return from the sheer overload inflicted upon them, and I feel a wetness in my pants. I groan. I've never actually been hit by a stun round before now, but I fired a few at pirates during boarding actions when I was a junior officer. About seven times out of ten, the person stunned suffers a very embarrassing release of the bladder. Apparently, I'm now one of the seven. This day just keeps getting better and better.

Good, you're finally awake." A face appears in my view, peering down at me. Owen isn't smiling or gloating; he's just looking at me with the same bored, almost disinterested expression he's mostly worn since I first met him.

I open my mouth to respond, but whatever comes out of it just sounds like a series of mumbles. So, I stop talking.

"You'll be fine in a few minutes, Brad, though I can't say the same for Jessica."

I yell this time, even though it's still incoherent, and I try to sit up but can't make my arms move.

Owen waits patiently for my unintelligible raving to stop. Then he raises his eyebrows and shrugs. "Sorry, Brad, but there have to be consequences when you disobey me. It's the only way we're going to have a productive working relationship. And that means hitting you where it hurts the worst—meaning Miss Lin."

My eyes frantically search the room, hoping beyond measure that I'll find Tucker there so I can confirm he's not with Jessica right now. Owen understands what I'm trying to do and shakes his head.

"Don't worry so much, Brad. I'm not a monster. Our dear Jessica has a couple of broken ribs courtesy of Jules. I'd never set Tucker loose on the poor woman unless…" He leaves the rest unsaid, but the implication is clear. And in that moment, so is my realization that I will do *anything* this man tells me to.

CHAPTER 11

The Job

When I'm recovered enough to walk, Owen has Tucker escort me to my quarters. The big man watches with an evil grin as I quickly shed my pee-soaked clothes and shower in the room's small bathroom. He forces me to leave the door open to make sure I'm not going for a weapon that I hid in the toilet or something. Then he pulls out a random shirt and pair of pants from my closet, demonstrating his complete lack of fashion sense as he pairs plaid with stripes. It would be funny if I weren't the one looking so ridiculous…and if my only friend and the woman I love weren't sitting under gunpoint somewhere, nursing cracked ribs or worse.

Finally, dressed like a clown—and definitely not appreciating the irony of that after my previous discussion on clowns with Jessica—I'm led back into the galley where Owen is waiting for me along with Harris, who at least still looks embarrassed for having shot me.

"Are you ready to tell me what's going on?" I growl as Tucker shoves me down into one of the seats surrounding the small table.

"Of course," Owen says, taking no notice of my tone. "You see, there is a man here in the Fiori system who has some information that my employer wants very much."

"And just who is your employer?" I interrupt.

Owen frowns and shakes his head. Then he picks up a small short-range comm that I hadn't noticed before and speaks into it. "Jules, it seems that Captain Mendoza needs another lesson. Go ahead and—"

"No!" I shout, trying to stand up but encountering a brick wall as Tucker shoves me back down in my seat. "I'll stop asking questions. Just don't hurt Jessica!"

Owen regards me coldly for a long moment, the radio still at his lips. Finally, he speaks again. "Jules, wait a bit. I think our dear captain is finally starting to grasp the realities of his situation."

He clicks off the comm without waiting for a response, leaving me irrationally worried that Jules didn't hear him and may even right now be hurting my first mate. But I hold it in, knowing that if I voice my concern or ask another question, then Jessica is *guaranteed* to be harmed further.

Owen seems to read my thoughts and nods once.

"Good man. Now, where was I? Oh yes, my employer wants the information this man has. And they are willing to pay me handsomely for retrieving it. But I cannot do so without your help. Which brings us to our present situation."

He pauses as if daring me to ask a question. When I don't, he continues. "The man in question, like you, is a member of the Promethean Navy. But he's offered to sell out his nation and share some very sensitive information with the Koratans for quite a lot of money. What I need from you, essentially, is to help us ID the man—you know, one Navy man recognizes the habits of another—and then convince him that *you're* the Koratan handler he's been told to expect. You'll get the information from him, give it to me, and then we'll all part ways as friends, with you another 4,500 credits richer. Any questions?"

I don't speak, sensing a trap. Owen sighs and shakes his head. "I mean it, Captain Mendoza. You can ask whatever you'd like now—within reason—and I promise Miss Lin won't be harmed."

"OK," I say slowly, not trusting this man's promises but also unwilling to upset him by not following his instructions. "What if he recognizes me? I'm not exactly an under-the-radar figure in the Promethean Navy."

"Terrific question," Owen says as if talking to an exceptionally bright preschooler. "And it's simple.

He served exclusively as an enlisted man in the Layton System Patrol. The chances that you ever crossed paths are minuscule, as your records show you were never stationed at Layton. Furthermore, just in case he recognizes you from the media firestorm around the Bellerophon disaster, Harris here is going to make you look much different than you do today. Any other questions?"

"Yes," I say hesitantly, not sure if I should take the risk. But I decide to push forward. "You said I need to help you ID the man. But you have his file, right? So why do you need me for that part?"

"Another good question. I suspected reports of your stupidity were exaggerated." If only he knew. "While the changes Harris will make to your appearance will be temporary, we have it on good authority that the man we're after has made some very permanent changes to his. We're talking extensive cosmetic surgery and enough bioengineering that even military-grade biometrics won't work to identify him. All paid for by the Koratans, of course, as part of their deal with him. He only agreed to give up the information they wanted after that was done. So, he's not a complete imbecile, even if he is a traitor."

He pauses again, inviting more questions.

"Where exactly is he?" I ask, hoping the answer is what I think it will be. Because I have the beginning of a plan forming in my head, but it will only work if this all goes down in a big public place…

"All we know is he's on the Rishi Paradise Casino Orbital above Fiori 2."

Jackpot!

I've never been to the Fiori system before. All I know about it now is the little I found and read on my implant while alone in the cockpit last night during Lin's turn to sleep. Since I never expected to visit this sector of human-controlled space, the information I had loaded was pretty sparse, but it might be enough.

For example, I know now that the system has a population of five billion spread across two inhabited planets. It's part of the Leeward Republic, a collection of relatively wealthy systems with a strong enough navy that not even the Federated Systems of Prometheus would dare upset them. And Fiori is no exception to that wealth. Especially since it's one of the rare systems that can boast more than one planet capable of supporting human life, meaning most of its five billion citizens are doing pretty well for themselves.

I also know that the system's biggest export is grain; one of the planets—Fiori 1—has incredibly fertile soil and fairly stable weather and seasonal variations. You can grow almost anything there, which they do. Then they sell it, for lots of money, to pretty much everyone else.

I also know that they have a supposedly democratic local government, that their national tree is something called a Fiori Fern—sounds pretty boring to me—and that their national bird is some kind of local animal that looks like a flying badger—not so boring

But that's about it. Oh, and I know that Fiori 2 isn't as fertile, at least not in terms of soil and weather. Instead, that planet's largest export is broke tourists who return home poorer from their stays in one of the planet's many orbital and surface-level casinos. And that, I hope, is how I'm going to get myself and Lin out of this mess.

"And the casino," I say to Owen, "has how many guests at any given time?"

He shrugs. "Five thousand, give or take."

"And you expect me to just saunter in there and find this guy out of five thousand people, right?"

"We do. As I said, we believe that as a Promethean Navy man yourself, you will be able to recognize patterns of behavior that we may otherwise miss." It's a dumb idea, but I'm not going to be the one to tell him that.

"And how much time do we have to find him?"

"Two standard days before his *real* Koratan handler shows up. We've managed to delay them, but only for that long. And *they* know what he looks like even with his new face. They did pay for it, after all."

"You know," I say, mentally crossing my fingers that this will work and not upset him again, "that what you're asking me to do is nearly impossible, right?"

He shrugs again. "I don't care how hard it is, Captain Mendoza. You will figure out how to do it, or Miss Lin will suffer the consequences. I trust in your resolve to do whatever it takes to keep her safe, if not in your ingenuity."

"Oh, I'll do it," I assure him. "But I can't do it alone."

His eyes narrow. "If you're suggesting that—"

I am suggesting what he's about to say, but I need to unbalance him a little before he can shut down the idea entirely. So, I take my biggest chance yet and interrupt him. "Do you know, Mr. Thompson, how to best draw out a Promethean Navy man? It's with a beautiful Promethean Navy woman. I guarantee you, if you let Jessica work with me on this one, your man will come to us."

He considers this for a long time, but I hold my tongue, not wanting to jinx it. That he doesn't immediately shoot down my idea is the best sign I've had yet in this conversation. Especially since I'm making this up as I go along and really have no idea how to accomplish what I just promised. But finally, almost as I'm about to lose my mind, Owen shrugs in that infuriatingly casual way he has. "Fine. Miss Lin can accompany you onto the station."

Uh oh. He gave in on that *way* too easily, and now I have to wait for the other shoe to drop...again.

CHAPTER 12

The Other Other Shoe

I don't have to wait very long this time. Within minutes, Jessica is brought to the galley, Jules again holding tight to her arm with a gun pressed into her ribs. By the pained look on my first mate's face, I can tell they're the same ribs the sadistic, shorter woman broke less than an hour before. It's all I can do not to punch Owen this time or leap across the room and try to kill Jules with my bare hands.

No, I need to stay calm now. It's our only hope… even if it means watching the woman I love suffer for a time.

Love stinks. Someone should write a song about that.

Shortly after Jules and Jessica enter the room, Owen motions to Harris, who gets up from his seat at the table and walks around behind the two women, his customary apologetic expression on his face. Before I can even ask what he intends, he reaches up and presses something to the back of Jessica's neck, and I hear her gasp in shock and pain.

"What did he do to her?" I ask, almost shouting, but I at least hold myself back from doing anything more rash than that, even if only barely this time.

Luckily, Owen seems to have anticipated this reaction and doesn't take it personally. Instead, he calmly explains. "Now, you didn't think I was going to just let you and Miss Lin disappear into a crowded casino with only your word that you'll do what I need you to do, did you?"

I absolutely hoped so; it was a critical part of my fledgling—and, in retrospect, stupid—plan. But I'm not going to give him the satisfaction of confirming it for him. He continues.

"What Mr. Harris has just injected into Miss Lin is a subdermal implant, though on a much smaller scale than the ones we all carry around in our brains. This one is rather dumb, in fact. It only does one thing, but it does it very well. If I don't send an hourly ping to it, it will trigger a small but very deadly explosive charge that will sever Miss Lin's spinal cord from the base of her brain, killing her instantly. Do you understand?"

I nod silently, not trusting my voice but not wanting to find out what he'll do if I refuse to answer. He seems satisfied with that, though I can see the horror in Jessica's eyes as she looks at me with a pleading stare. I force myself to look away from her and back at Owen, whose expression still looks bored.

"Good then," he says. "We understand each other. One important note. Try to dig the implant out, it will explode. Try to tamper with it in any way, it will explode. And since the casino has a dampening field to prevent cheating amongst players, I can only reset it if I have line-of-sight to Miss Lin."

"What about when she needs to sleep?" I ask, instantly regretting the query.

"Now that's a dumb question," Owen says, then nods at Jules.

Jessica screams in pain as Jules pulls back the hand with the gun and then jabs it fast and hard back into my friend's already busted ribs. This time, it's too much for me, and I do leap toward them, only to have Tucker's iron fist explode against the side of my head, dropping me to the deck. Thankfully, I don't lose control of my consciousness or my bladder this time.

"Even though it was a dumb question," Owen says, a hardness to his tone that wasn't there before, "I'll answer it. You only have two standard days —49 hours, to be exact—before mission failure. If I were you, I wouldn't even *think* about spending any of that time sleeping. We will provide you with a room to refresh yourselves and change clothes, but at least one of us will be there at all times so that you can't use it to conspire against us or do anything else to jeopardize the mission. And if you somehow still manage to be just as much an idiot as the media reports suggest you are, then the cost will be Jessica Lin's life. Do I make myself clear?"

This time, I sense a simple nod won't suffice. "Crystal," I say from the hard deck where I still sit after Tucker's punch. And I see Owen Thompson smile broadly for the first time.

It's not something I ever hope to see again.

CHAPTER 13

Rishi Paradise

Owen lied when he said we would have forty-nine hours to find our target. We burn six of those hours just getting to the Rishi Paradise Casino Orbital (say that five times fast) and two more hours waiting for a docking slip. Apparently, the place is wildly popular.

So now, as Jessica and I enter the station, with Owen and his cronies right behind us, we only have forty-one of those hours left.

Our first stop is the cashier's office at the front of the casino, where Owen procures various denominations of chips representing currency since we can't use our implants inside the casino itself.

Our second stop, at my insistence, is a clothing boutique in the casino's shopping center. There, I procure a few things that we'll need. Anything to get myself out of the plaid and stripes that

Tucker put me in. I also explain to Jessica what I'm planning and have her pick something for herself. She's silent throughout the process, and I'm worried about her, but Owen doesn't give us any chance to be alone so I can't try and talk to her about it.

We reach the register with our new clothes, and I raise an eyebrow at Owen. He frowns, but he's obviously impressed with my genetic ability to raise a single eyebrow because he steps forward and pays the bill using some of his chips. Which is good because Jessica's new dress would have eaten deeply into the 4,500 sitting in our bank account.

The next stop is the check-in desk, where Owen gives the reservation details to a pretty blond who is dressed in a toga, of all things. Apparently, the Rishi Paradise has some sort of weird neo-Roman theme. Parts of the station interior are even decorated with fake stone pillars interspersed with bright neon lights. It looks horribly cheesy and cheap to me, but based on the dress of the other patrons and the prices we—well, Owen—paid at the clothing store, I'm guessing that Rishi caters to a more upscale clientele.

That's good, in a way. It should make our Navy enlisted man stand out like a sore thumb. Still a sore thumb that we have to find in a crowd of five thousand other thumbs, but I'll take what I can get.

The good news is that there's no chance the guy

will recognize me, even if he watched my court martial live on a huge screen or has a poster of me above his bed. Harris is that good. He spent a significant portion of the remaining flight to Rishi going over both Lin and me with a wide variety of tools, liquids, gels, and gadgets. I hardly recognized myself in the mirror afterward. I have blond hair now, and my cheekbones are more pronounced. Even my eye color has changed.

Jessica looks more like herself; the chances our target might have ever seen a picture of her are far lower since she's not a mass murderer like me. But the goal with her, per the plan I explained to Owen, is to actually make her stand out. We *want* our man to notice her. According to Owen, our target has never met his Koratan handler and doesn't even know their gender. So, my brilliant plan is to make him think *Jessica* is the handler, not me.

That means I need her to be noticeable because I'm banking that a lowly enlisted man will be expecting this spy stuff to happen like it does in books and movies, not in boring real life. And every good spy movie has a stunning femme fatale, right? Sure, it's a stupid plan, but I haven't exactly been given all that much to work with.

We finally arrive at the room Owen arranged for us. He and his entire entourage accompany us inside. At least they let us go into the bathroom to change our clothes in private, but only one at a time, and after Tucker has checked the room for anything that can be used as a weapon. Which is too bad; I was really hoping the prior occupant left behind a crowbar or a Series T-1000 laser assault rifle. At this point, I'd even take a particularly sharp toothpick.

I go first, and I have to admit, I like the new suit I've purchased for myself. It has a lot of pockets, something that was always lacking in Navy-issue skinsuits. I don't have anything to put in those pockets, but just knowing they're there gives me a sliver of happiness despite our situation.

But when Jessica emerges from the bathroom a few minutes later, I lose all interest in my pockets.

Up until now, I've only seen Jessica Lin in two types of clothing. First, her Navy skinsuit, which, despite being very flattering to her figure, didn't exactly go for aesthetics otherwise. Second, a series of casual outfits, mostly simple pants and t-shirts, during our time on *Wanderer*. After all, Heather Kilgore didn't provide us with a whole lot of variety, though I was pleasantly surprised to find she had somehow magically stocked *Wanderer* with at least a few clothes in both our sizes.

But now...I've never seen anything more breathtaking. The dress Lin picked out in the boutique is bright red with lines woven into the fabric that shimmer and catch the light as she walks. It has a slit up the side, though not too high, leaving plenty to the imagination. The top of the dress is sleeveless but actually quite modest. Nevertheless, the way it hangs on her accentuates every one of her curves and makes my mouth drop open in awe. As she walks toward me in the small room, I'm having a hard time remembering that we're fighting for our lives here.

I mean, Jessica Lin would look amazing in a garbage bag. But this is a whole new level of beauty that I didn't even know existed.

Despite that, Harris isn't happy. In my efforts to make Jessica stand out more, I'd had the man turn her hair a bright blue on the voyage in. Now, he's dissatisfied with the way it clashes with the red dress. I expect Owen to tell him to drop it, but surprisingly, the man lets his minion work. It only takes fifteen minutes and a strange electronic doodad that I've never seen before today, and then Jessica's hair and dress match perfectly. I have to admit, for a guy who dresses like a hobo, Harris knows his way around cosmetics and fashion.

"Wait," he says as Jessica turns to walk away from him and the hotel room's small vanity. And from nowhere, he produces jewelry.

In the Navy, women don't wear jewelry. You don't wear anything that can get stuck on a vacsuit or helmet. Not if you want to live. But somehow, Jessica dons the diamond studded bracelet, choker, and earrings that Harris produces like she's born to them. And I suddenly realize that I don't really know all that much about her background before the Navy. For all I know, her parents were insanely wealthy, and she wore jewelry like this to grade school.

I will tell you this: if I wasn't already in love with this woman, I would fall hopelessly now. But seeing her this way at this moment is actually quite depressing because I know there's no chance for us to be together, even assuming we survive the next forty hours.

CHAPTER 14

Searching in Vain

Fifteen minutes after Harris pronounces us both good to go, Jessica and I walk arm-in-arm through the hotel lobby and into the casino proper of the Rishi Paradise. Somewhere behind us are Owen, Harris, Tucker, and Jules, but they're far enough away that they can't hear. And the blanket jamming that the casino uses to dissuade cheating means that they can't listen in even if they've planted microphones on us, which I don't think they could have. That's the other reason I purchased new clothes for us and then never let those clothes out of my sight until we got them on.

I just have to hope that Owen is right about him still being able to get a signal to Jessica's new and terrible implant, as long as he has line-of-sight to her. Otherwise, she'll be dead within an hour. Cheery thought.

But I can't worry about that now, as much as

it tears at my heart, because I need to focus on the few things I *can* control. For now, that means doing everything I can to complete our impossible mission successfully, which means adding one more accessory to her outfit.

"Here," I tell her once we've entered the noisy casino floor. I hand her a small silver pin.

She looks down at it in her hand. "You're joking, right?" Harris put lash extensions on her and a shimmering dark eye shadow that makes her eyes 'pop'. That's the word he used, but it fits because even now, looking at me with incredulity, those eyes are amazing.

"Hey, why not?" I ask.

"Because it's too obvious. There's no way the guy falls for it," she argues.

"Trust me, one look at you, and he'll be willing to believe just about anything for an excuse to get close. And this will be like a beacon to him."

She frowns but doesn't argue further, though she does decline my offer to help her pin the thing on.

"There," she says once it's securely fashioned to her dress right above her left breast. "Happy?"

"Yep," I try and say nonchalantly, but it catches in my throat and sounds more like a frog croaking. Real smooth, Brad.

The pin, small though it is, is unmistakable to anyone who knows anything about Fringe navies.

"Where did you get this anyway?" Lin asks as I start to lead her through the casino again.

"I took it off the body of a Koratan officer I killed in hand-to-hand combat."

She stops dead in her tracks, yanking her arm out of mine and folding it with the other across her chest. "Brad, stop it," she hisses. "I need to know you're taking this seriously. Our lives are on the line!" A few patrons look our way as Lin's voice rises loud enough to be heard, but I smile and nod at them as if it's all some big joke, and they quickly go back to their slot machines and keno games. Except for a few old guys who keep staring at Jessica, but it's hard to blame them.

"Sorry," I say, offering my arm back to her. She takes it, but only after hesitating a moment longer than I would have liked. "I make jokes when I'm nervous. And when I'm hungry. And when I'm—"

"Brad," she hisses again. I take the hint.

"Sorry. Again. I won the pin in a poker game on the Harper Line."

The Harper Line is a sort of neutral zone between Promethean and Koratan space. Both nations claim the three inhabited systems there, and they regularly send their respective navies through to patrol them and show the flag. But someone forgot to tell the inhabitants of those three systems that they belong to either nation. So, what you essentially get is disputed territory where the denizens cater equally to both nations' navies. Add on top of that the fact that few people in those navies actually want to get into a shooting war with each other, and you end up with a sort of uneasy and unspoken truce on the Line. Sometimes, you even find a good underground poker game where you can rub shoulders with officers from the opposite side of our little cold war.

She accepts my answer this time, which is good because it's the truth, and I feel her relax, but only slightly. She's still wound so tightly she could probably *push* the *Wanderer* to the next system over.

"Listen," I tell her, "I'm working on a plan, but I need that brilliant mind of yours. The best thing we can do until we come up with something better is to find the guy Owen is looking for and get whatever information from him that Owen's employer wants. Then, hopefully, we can get out of this system and away from him and the rest of them and never look back."

She's silent for a while, walking beside me, and I'm trying very hard not to be too conscious of her arm through mine. When she speaks again, I have to strain to hear her near whisper. "That's if they're telling the truth about letting us go when this is over."

She has me there because I'm almost certain

they're not. Especially because I'm starting to get a pretty strong suspicion of who Owen's mysterious employer likely is.

But, without anything else to do until we come up with something better, and needing very badly for Owen to keep sending his hourly signal to Jessica's new implant, we have no choice but to look for the traitor from our old Navy.

So, we keep walking around the casino floor, hoping vainly that some guy sees Jessica and notices the pin on her chest and pops up and yells, 'Hey, I'm the traitor you're looking for'. He doesn't. And after six *hours* of walking around, sometimes with Jessica alone out in front—which has *every* guy in the casino trying to talk to her—and sometimes arm-in-arm—which has every guy in the casino giving me dirty looks—I have to admit defeat.

We only have thirty-three hours left.

CHAPTER 15

*A New Approach and
a Fantastic Failure*

"I'm hungry," I announce as we finish our latest full circuit around the casino floor.

"Really?" Jessica says next to me. We're arm-in-arm again; it was slowing us down way too much to have to stop when she got hit on every five meters. "How can you even think of food at a time like this?"

"I can always think of food," I say, and then drag her toward one of the many restaurants placed around the edges of the casino. This one is a bar and grill, and I feel Jessica pull against me as we near it. By our ship's clock, it's breakfast time. By Rishi's, it's just after the lunch rush, and the place is only half full.

"No, Brad, this is *not* the time," Lin says harshly, and I'm a little disappointed. Does she really think

I would drink again right in front of her? No, I'd only do that behind her back.

"Relax," I tell her, though Carla used to tell me that was one of five words a man should never say to a woman. But I'm a slow learner, and Carla isn't here. She's with Clarington, hopefully crying into his pudgy shoulder about my death.

I shake off thoughts of my ex-wife. It's easy to do that with Jessica Lin on my arm. "Relax," I say again. "I'm not going to drink anything. But you know what they say about station bars?"

She doesn't reply, but her resistance stops, and she lets me lead her into the restaurant, where a cute little hostess, also in a toga, leads us to a table. After she finishes telling us about the day's specials, I do my best to casually ask my planned question.

"Say, we're trying to meet up with a friend here at the casino, but we can't message him with the comm jamming. Any chance you may have seen him?"

The hostess looks at me with an expression that says, 'Do you know how many people I see daily? I'm going to forget you exist the second you let me leave this table'. But I forge ahead anyway.

"You'd recognize him. Ex-Navy guy. Probably telling all sorts of stories about his time serving over in Prometheus. Ring any bells?"

"What's he look like?" she asks. Shoot, the most obvious question but also the one question I can't answer. Luckily, Jessica saves me.

"So, this is a little embarrassing," she tells the hostess. "He's more a friend of a friend. We've never actually met him. All we know is that he's here this week, and our mutual friend said he could hook us up with some concert tickets we've been after for months."

The hostess nods dubiously but doesn't argue, and luckily doesn't ask the guy's name, because we don't know that either. "Doesn't remind me of anyone we've had through here. Sorry I can't help you."

I'm about to shrug it off when something hits my shin hard. I yelp, drawing a surprised look from the hostess, but I quickly figure out it was one of the high heels Jessica bought to go with her new dress; couldn't have her wearing her normal combat boots with that little ensemble. And Jess is looking at me now and motioning with her head toward the server. I look back in confusion, but then I finally get it.

"Well, if you do hear or see anyone who you think matches the description, please let us know." I hand her one of the twenty credit chips Owen gave me for walking around money while we search for our target.

The girl brightens and looks far more helpful now.

"I'll definitely let you know. You may also ask some of the other staff. This is my first day back on station from a trip down planet, so they may have seen your friend while I was gone."

Great! Couldn't she have led with that? I just spent twenty credits on someone who has no chance of helping us.

"Thank you so much," Jessica says graciously, and the toga-clad girl bounces off back to the hostess station.

"Ow," I say once she's out of earshot as I reach down to rub my bruised shin. "What are those shoes made out of, hull metal?"

"You should try wearing the blasted things for the last six hours," Jessica says as she surveys the other diners around us. "That's real torture."

"Really? My ex-wife always said she liked wearing them." Another smooth move by Brad Mendoza. Here I am, sitting with the most beautiful woman in the galaxy, and I bring up my ex-wife. Nice. Maybe next I can tell her all about my last colonoscopy.

"No one actually enjoys wearing high heels," Jessica says, ignoring or perhaps even oblivious to my faux pas. "It's just something women pretend they like to please men."

"But," I argue, "Carla wore them long before she met me. And she kept wearing them even after I told her I didn't care. She was always buying new ones."

She looks at me now, breaking off her study of the other people in the restaurant. "Brad, sometimes you really are dense, aren't you?"

Her words are harsh, but there's no real bite to them. So, they don't hurt as much as when she called me an idiot just a few days ago.

"Enlighten me," I challenge her.

"OK," she turns her body more directly toward me in her chair as if settling in for an intense conversation. We're both just trying to distract ourselves from our current situation, but that's not such a bad thing. "How long were you and Carla married?"

"Six years."

"And in those six years, how often were you actually together, like in the same apartment or house, on the same planet."

I think for a moment. "Well, with my deployment schedule, I guess maybe only a quarter of the time."

"OK, so about a year-and-a-half of actual time together then?"

"Sounds about right."

"And when did you first catch her cheating on you?"

"Wait, how did you know that? I've never told anyone." I don't like how this conversation is going at all.

"Just answer the question, Brad."

"Three months after Bellerophon," I admit.

"And what did she do when you were on deployment? Did she sit around and pine for you in your apartment?"

"We had a house."

"Whatever. Answer the question."

"Well, no. She had a group of girlfriends she would go out with. But I was OK with it. They would just go to movies and stuff."

"Now. And this is important. How many pairs of high heels did she have?"

"Uh. A lot. Maybe twenty. Maybe more."

"You said she was always buying more. But did she ever throw any out because they were too worn or scuffed?"

I think hard, struggling to remember. "I think so. Yes, I'm certain. There were always new pairs when I'd get home, but I remember a few of my favorites—the ones I thought looked best on her—would be gone. I just figured she wanted to keep her wardrobe fresh."

"OK, last question. These friends of hers that she would go out with while you were on deployment.

Did they ever hang out with her while you were around? I mean, did they come over to the house while you were there, or did she go out with them while you were in town?"

"Uh. No. Now that you mention it, I met a few of them at our wedding but never really saw them after that."

Her facial expression changes to a pained one. "Oh, you dear, sweet, stupid man. I'm so sorry."

"What? What are you sorry about?" I demand, sick of playing twenty questions and being called stupid. A few other diners look our way at my outburst.

"Brad, I hate to break it to you, but that time you caught Carla cheating on you…I'm pretty sure it wasn't her first time." She stops, letting that sink in.

"No, you're wrong," I argue, again a bit too loudly. "Carla was loyal. There's no way she was cheating on me before…" But I can't finish the sentence because, all of a sudden, things start falling into place. Three months before I caught Carla in bed with Clarington, the man had attended my court martial. I thought it was just because his daddy, the Vice Admiral Clarington, was one of the judges on the panel. But now I recall that I caught him staring at me a lot and nudging some of his friends and laughing as if there was some great joke at my expense.

Then, I remember a time before that when I got home from deployment a day early and thought it would be fun to surprise Carla instead of telling her my new schedule. I caught a cab home. Just as it pulled up and I was getting out, another car drove past the house slowly. At first, it looked as if it was actually going to turn into my driveway. But instead, as it got closer, the driver hit the accelerator and sped by.

When I went inside, I found Carla waiting by the front door, resplendent in a black dress I'd always loved on her, with spiky black heels to match.

The funny part was, looking back, she seemed genuinely surprised to see me but then made a big deal about how she had dressed up to welcome me home. When, disappointed at my failed surprise, I asked her how she even knew I was coming home early, she'd said, "Daddy told me."

The thing is, Admiral Oliphant had no idea I was coming home early. It wasn't planned, but my transport caught a rogue gravitational wave in jump space and rode it for several dozen lightyears, cutting an entire day off our travel time to Prometheus. When we arrived, Terrence Oliphant was in the outer system doing combat training exercises with First Fleet. Even if he had gotten the news that the transport had arrived early, he wouldn't have been able to get a message back to Carla until almost half a day after I actually walked in the front door.

Which means she wasn't waiting for *me* dressed like that.

Everything clicks into place now, and I feel hot tears well up in my eyes.

"I'm so sorry, Brad," Jessica says, reaching out to place one of her hands on top of mine. Usually, any kind of physical contact from her would electrify me, but not this, not now. "I'm so sorry. I figured you must know. I just assumed that was part of why you got divorced."

I jerk my hand back, not sure how to react to anything right now. She looks hurt for a moment, but it passes quickly.

"Listen," she tries to change the subject, "the idea of asking the staff here for information on our man is a good one. Let's keep throwing some of those chips around and see what it gets us."

I still say nothing, staring down at the table in front of me, reading the same line on the menu over and over again without remembering a single word, and fighting hard to keep the tears from falling. It feels like someone punched me in the gut and then pulled the floor out from beneath me.

"Brad, I'm so sorry. Maybe when this is all over, we can talk more about what a real, healthy relationship looks like."

Well, it's been a few hours since the last truly stupid thing I've done, so I'm due. But what I say next is perhaps the most monumentally dumb thing to ever leave my lips. I mean, we are talking Nobel Prize-level idiocy on this one.

"Like you would know."

I whisper the words, but Jessica hears them. She stiffens across from me, and a stricken look clouds her perfect features. Then, wordlessly, she pulls the napkin off her lap, folds it carefully, and places it on the table in front of her. She then deliberately and carefully pushes her chair back and stands up.

My mind is racing now as I realize what I've done, and I open my mouth to plead my case, apologize, anything! But the words just won't come. Instead, I watch mutely as Jessica turns and then walks briskly from the restaurant, leaving me behind. Every man in the place follows her with their gaze as she does so.

What. An. Idiot. But I guess I should stop expecting more from myself.

Our waitress picks that very moment to arrive, another bouncy little blond in a toga. There's a definite hiring trend at this casino.

"Is everything OK with your wife, sir?" she asks in feigned concern.

I shake my head slowly. "Just bring me your biggest bottle of scotch."

CHAPTER 16

Success, But at What Cost?

Usually, after such a monumental act of sheer idiocy, I can't wait to erase my memory, at least temporarily, with copious amounts of alcohol.

I expect now to be no different, but twenty minutes later, I still sit here, staring at the glass of scotch in my hand, the one I first poured, that I haven't even taken a sip of.

There are so many things going through my head right now, few of them good. But one keeps coming back to the surface: if I get drunk now, Jessica Lin is a dead woman. With only thirty-three hours left, I can't afford to spend even a few hours of that time drunk and useless. And once I take one sip, I won't stop. Still, I *need* the drink so badly. So, I just sit there, unable to make up my mind, staring into its amber depths.

I'm in this state of startling conundrum when

Owen slips into the chair Jessica vacated.

"What happened?" he asked.

Seeing him here, I frantically access my implant to check the time.

"Relax," he says, picking up on what I'm doing. "She's at the bar two doors down. I pinged her little implant before I walked over here to see what in Hades is wrong with you. She's got fifty-seven minutes before I need to ping it again."

I nod, not sure if it's appropriate to thank the man for not killing the woman I love. So, I say nothing. Instead, I give the glass of scotch one last fond gaze before I get up, leaving the glass and the bottle untouched on the table behind me, and walk in the direction Jessica went. I'll let Owen settle my bill.

I find her right where he said she'd be. Unlike the restaurant we were in, which was a bar pretending to be a grill with fancy food, this new establishment makes no such pretenses. It's just a bar, and the waitresses here wear togas even shorter and more revealing than any I've yet seen. It's also dark, and there's smoke in the air from several of the patrons who haven't been able to kick a habit that was proved to be deadly hundreds or perhaps even thousands of years ago.

She's sitting alone at the bar, an empty shot glass in front of her, which she's staring into and studying as if it holds the key to our predicament. Or maybe she's trying to forget what just happened between us. But I know better. All the booze in the world doesn't wipe away the memories we most desperately wish it would. Those are here to stay.

I stand there and watch her for a few minutes, unsure of how to proceed. In that time, three different men approach her. She sends the first away with nothing more than a cold look. The second, she sends scurrying onward with just a few words. But the third is more persistent. I'm about to go intervene, but the guy's hand on her lower back quickly results in her bending his finger so far back that I can almost hear it crack from across the bar. I admire her work as the third guy scampers past me out of the bar, holding his hurt hand in the other and swearing. She doesn't even watch him go.

When I slide onto the stool next to her a moment later, she looks up as if to tell another would-be Romeo to buzz off. But when she sees it's me, she says nothing and looks down at her empty drink again.

For several more minutes, neither of us says anything. But I can feel the angry glances of every other single guy in the bar directed at my back. If only they knew that she likely hates me more than even the guy she just sent running to a first aid station.

Finally, I work up the courage to speak. "Listen, Jessica, I'm—"

"I found him," she says, interrupting what I was hoping would be a truly heartfelt and heartstring-tugging apology from yours truly. But the moment is over, and now I'm no longer seeing Jessica Lin, the woman I love and who laughed with me and told stories in the *Wanderer's* cockpit. Instead, I'm seeing Lieutenant Commander Lin, the woman who, on the second day after we met—hard to believe that was less than two weeks ago—dressed me down for staring at her butt.

I'm afraid I've lost the other Lin forever. This one is all business now.

"Where? How?" I ask, letting myself forlornly slip back into my role as Captain Brad Mendoza, her superior officer who will almost certainly never be anything more.

"The bartender," she motions with her head, still refusing to look at me. I look over to see a tall brunette woman—finally someone who breaks the casino's staffing mold—cleaning a glass two meters away and flirting unabashedly with a couple of older men who keep flicking casino chips her way while simultaneously casting furtive glances toward Jessica. I can see from here that at least one is wearing a wedding ring. Real nice.

Funny, even after so many years among the stars, sometimes it doesn't feel like we as humans have evolved, not even a little bit. And I include myself in that.

"She says a guy was in here just last night," Jessica continues. "Got a couple of drinks in him and started bragging about being some big shot in the Promethean Navy. Tells this tall tale about being a daring captain who took out six pirate ships with a single battlecruiser."

"Hey, that's my story," I say despite myself. She doesn't acknowledge that I've even spoken.

"She says we can usually find him at one of the craps tables. He's blond with blue eyes and a chiseled jaw. Guess he was going for a look that he thought would get him more girls. Supposedly, he also wears a red rose in his lapel. She thought he was full of it and that he talked way too rough to have actually been an officer in any navy, but he was pretty liberal with the chips he was throwing her way, so she kept him talking."

With that, Jessica gets up to leave, and I scramble to follow. She tosses a chip on the bar for the bartender's trouble, then walks briskly out the door. I'm a few steps behind, but the opportunity —however brief—I had to apologize to her is now gone and over.

As is any opportunity for a future between Brad Mendoza and Jessica Lin. Because even I have to admit, if I were her, after all she's been through, I would never forgive me for what I said.

CHAPTER 17

Finding Our Man

Now that we have a description, our guy is surprisingly easy to find. He's not at the craps tables, but he is right next to them, playing blackjack and losing quite badly, both at the game and with the pretty dealer he's clumsily flirting with.

As we get close, Jessica throws me a hard look, stopping me in my tracks. She continues forward, leaving me behind. That hurts more than anything else she could have said or done because she just made it clear that she no longer trusts me with her life. She's going to handle this herself or die trying rather than put any faith in me.

I sit, dejectedly, at another table where I can see the one our target is at. I mindlessly bet and lose a few hands as I watch Jessica at work, perhaps for the last time.

She's good. I have to give her that. She slides into

the seat next to the guy. He looks her over, his eyes lingering in all the right places, but she pretends not to notice. Instead, she places some of Owen's chips on the table and asks to be dealt in.

I see the exact moment the guy notices the pin on her chest. It takes him a little while because it's on the side opposite him, but when he finally sees it, he goes rigid. After all, no one is expecting to see the Koratan Medal of Valor on a supermodel, especially this far from Koratan space.

He's still staring at it when the dealer literally has to tap him on the arm to get his attention. He mumbles something at her, and she shrugs, dealing him another card. He busts. So do I, by the way. At this rate, I'll lose my remaining chips faster than Lin can land this fish.

But I don't have to wait long. He leans over urgently and asks her something. She pretends to notice him for the first time but places a hand gently on his arm and shushes him, like a teacher to a naughty student. It works. Sort of. He plays a few more hands, but he's shaking so badly and so distracted that he's just making random moves, and he busts quickly on two hands and then holds at nine on the third. The pile of chips in front of him is almost gone.

Lin chooses that moment to lean over and whisper something in his ear. He stiffens again but nods. Then she gets up, tosses a chip to the dealer, collects the rest of hers, and walks away slowly. The guy stays put for only a few seconds, nervously bouncing, until he gets up and follows my first mate—if she's even that anymore. But before he does, Jessica catches my eye and indicates through sheer anger that I'm to follow after him as he follows after her.

I get the message. I collect my own chips, toss one to the dealer at my table, and try to follow the target as casually as I can. Not that he would notice me even if I shouted in his ear. Between his nervous energy at finally making contact with his supposed handler and the fact that he can't take his eyes off Jessica's rear end—I've been there, buddy—a battleship would have to *hit* him for him to even notice it approaching.

She leads him to a relatively quiet restaurant, not one of the two we've already been in, gets a table, and invites him to sit with her. He's still bouncing. I wait outside; there's clearly not a third seat for me anyway. And frankly, I don't think she needs any help with this guy.

They talk quietly for a few minutes, breaking off only when the waiter—I didn't think the casino employed men—dressed like a Roman gladiator arrives to take their order.

I find a bench outside where I can see into the restaurant and keep an eye on things. I'm still there five minutes later, watching Jessica work from a distance, when Owen plops down beside me.

"Good job finding him," he says without preamble. "Now, let's hope your girl can seal the deal."

"She's not my girl," I say in return, not really wanting to put up with the guy's fake friendly crap for one more second.

"You know what I mean," he says calmly.

I look over at him now, meeting his eyes and staring so hard I hope I'll make his head explode. "Shut up, Owen." Then I get up and walk away.

CHAPTER 18

The Wrinkle

"What do you mean it's not here?"

It's the first time I've seen Owen look genuinely angry since the time he snapped at Tucker outside *Wanderer*. But Jessica doesn't react. She wears the same impassive, stony expression that's been on her face since the moment I finished putting my gigantic foot in my mouth back at the first restaurant we went into.

"Just as I said," she explains calmly. "The information isn't here. The guy isn't a total fool, after all. He wants payment first, then he'll give us the location of the dead drop where he left the intel you want."

I now have the pleasure of watching Owen Thompson sputter and throw his hands up in the air in frustration and anger. It's a good look on him. I hope to see him frustrated more often moving forward, so long as it isn't directed at us.

There's still that nasty little implant in Jessica's neck to consider.

Owen paces the hotel room where we've all met up again, muttering to himself. Finally, he stops and looks hard at me.

"Fix it," he says simply and definitively.

"What do you expect *me* to do?" I argue. "Just pay the guy, and you'll get what you're after." I don't even mention the fact that he should be talking to Jess, not me. *She's* the one who found the target; I don't feel like I've contributed much at all to this little mission. But better to keep the psychopath's focus off her and on me, I suppose.

"No." Owen says the word with such finality that it's not even worth arguing with him. I do, anyway.

"What do you mean, no? You told us to find the guy; we found him. Now she's telling you exactly how you can get the intel you're after from him. So just pay him, and we can all part ways happy."

"No," he says again, and he steps forward and jabs one of his sausage-like fingers in my chest. Behind him, I see Tucker smirk at me from where he sits on one of the room's beds. Harris and Jules are nowhere to be seen. "I told you to find him *and* get the intel for me. So, find me a way to get what we came for that doesn't involve me paying the guy twenty million credits."

Now, *that* catches my attention. On the flight in,

Owen told me the guy was selling his intel for a lot of money, but *twenty million credits*? For that much, it has to be some explosively valuable information. But what could be so valuable to the Koratans that a lowly in-system spacer would know...?

I want to moan out loud when it hits me. Because suddenly, I'm pretty sure I know exactly what information the guy has. And it's not good. But the real question is, do I care?

And the answer is yes. But not because I care who actually gets such valuable intel. For all I'm concerned, King Charles, Lord and Ruler of the Federated Systems of Prometheus and uncle to a rapist, can rot. But I can't do anything that will put Jessica in more danger. And until we find a way to remove that explosive implant, that means I need to keep playing Owen's little game.

"Fine," I say through clenched teeth. "We'll find another way."

CHAPTER 19

The Other Way

Did you know implants are really spectacular devices? I remember hearing once, maybe in school, that the average implant can hold the entirety of what the internet contained a thousand years ago. Not bad for something small enough to fit in your head. Of course, as storage grows, so does the amount of information available, so we still have to be choosy about what we store in our implants. They can run out of space. But the space they do have is still astonishingly large.

For example, in my role as a captain in His Majesty's Promethean Navy, I've long had my implant set to automatically download any and all naval bulletins every time I come in range of a planetary internet node. Usually, I don't bother reading any unless my implant's AI tells me one of them has a direct impact on me or my ship. But included in those bulletins are alerts for any spacers or officers who occasionally go AWOL or otherwise disappear. And I have these bulletins stored in perpetuity, going back several years, last updated just eight days ago when I was in Gerson.

Owen told us that our target deserted from his duty station in the Layton system, where he served as part of the system patrol. But the funny thing is, I can't find a single bulletin in my implant about *anyone* deserting or going AWOL from Layton in the last five years.

But there *has* been a recently AWOL spacer from another system, and it confirms a suspicion I've had since the moment Owen revealed he knew our true identities. It also means that now I have a real plan to end this.

I quickly explain a portion of that plan, without revealing what I've learned from the records in my implant, to Owen, Jessica, and the rest. Then, I sit impatiently for thirty minutes while Harris undoes most of the changes he made to my appearance. My cheekbones are still a little too pronounced, but at least my hair and eyes are back to their proper coloring.

Even with all that, I'm ten minutes early to the place where Jessica arranged to meet our target, who told her his name is Jorge. He's already there, of course. When a woman like Jessica Lin tells you to meet her somewhere, you show up early to ensure there's *no* chance you miss your rendezvous.

I slip into the seat across from the traitor, who is too busy looking all around for Jessica to even notice me approaching.

"Uh," he says in confusion when he finally sees me there. "I'm expecting someone."

"Not anymore, Jorge," I say, channeling some of the bored psychopath tone that I've learned to love so much from good old Owen.

"I, uh, don't understand," he responds haltingly.

"That's because you're not thinking hard enough, Jorge," I say, this time a bit derisively. "Or, should I say, George Peterson?"

OK. I hate Owen, and I'd love to kill him and all his friends at this point. But I get it now: the big reveal he did in the galley when he told me he knew my real name. I get why he did it that way because the look on Jorge's face is absolutely priceless.

"How did you know?" he asks, his whisper way too loud.

"Come on, George," I say with a lopsided grin. "Don't you recognize me?"

His eyes search my face for several long seconds, and I can see it isn't ringing any bells with him. I sigh internally; I guess I'm not as famous as I thought, which is a major blow to my ego. It's the cheekbones that Harris couldn't fully undo. That must be it, right?

"Think Butcher of Bellaraphon," I say reluctantly.

That does it. His eyes go wide with recognition, and his mouth falls open in surprise. I do that a lot, too—the whole jaw dropping open when something surprises me—but seeing it now on another person, mouth agape like he's a whale after krill, makes me want to rethink ever using it again.

"You're Brad Mendoza!" Several heads turn at other tables, responding to his proclamation. Idiot.

"Keep your voice down, George," I hiss. "You know, you make a really crappy spy."

"But you're…" he starts to exclaim again but stops himself. "But you're dead," he says in what he probably thinks is a whisper, but to me, still sounds like rushing wind in a thunderstorm.

"Apparently not," I say.

"But how?"

"Come on, George. Hero captain with spotless record accidentally kills 504 civilians, then mysteriously dies in a place like Gerson? You don't really believe all of that, do you?"

"I… Wait, you mean it was all an act?" I love it when useful fools fill in the blanks for me.

I don't respond but raise my eyebrows, inviting him to keep speculating.

"But why?" Oh well. Seems like I'll need to do the heavy lifting for him.

"It's quite simple, really. I'm part of ProSec now."

If he looked shocked earlier at my identity, his shock doubles now. The blood drains from his face because, for a spy and traitor against the Federated Systems of Prometheus, the Promethean Security Service—'ProSec' for short—is his worst nightmare. It means he's been caught.

Oh, sure, he doesn't give up immediately. He stammers for a while, trying to explain his new appearance, what he's doing so far from his duty station, etc., etc., etc. But as he does so, he also lets slip a lot of very useful information, all of which makes me feel a whole lot better because it's more or less exactly what I expected. Then, it makes me feel a lot worse because it's more or less *exactly* what I expected. And what I expected is pretty scary. It means the stakes of the game Jessica and I are unwillingly playing in are as high as they can possibly get.

Finally, as he runs out of wind and lies to tell, I chime back in. "Listen very carefully, George, because you are in grave danger."

He looks like he wants to say something, but I don't wait for him to ask any stupid questions.

"That woman you met with earlier; she's not who you think. She was sent here to kill you."

His mouth drops open again, and this time, he reminds me of a fish I once caught. Yep, I definitely need a new go-to facial expression when I'm surprised.

"In fact," I continue, "the Koratans have been planning to kill you all along after you give them the intel you stole. You simply know too much for them to allow you to live."

It's all very believable to him because everything he knows about spies comes from movies and novels, just as I suspected. I can see it in the way he reacts. But, in reality, the Koratans probably aren't going to actually kill him; that would mean way too much paperwork. They're far more likely to put him in some secret prison somewhere and let him get killed by another prisoner. Cleaner that way.

"What do I do?" he asks, again too loudly, leaning across the table toward me.

"Well, you have two choices, George. First, you come with me. You take me to wherever you've stashed the information you were going to sell the Koratans; I suspect you're way too smart to have brought it to this meeting, right?"

He nods vigorously.

"Great. You take me to it, you give it to me, I give you a new identity, and you go on your merry way."

I pause, waiting. Finally, as anticipated, he breaks the silence. "And the second option?"

I lean back and smile, showing my teeth. "The

second option is to see whether the pretty Koratan assassin or I get to kill you first. Because you screwed up George. By hiding the info where only you can find it, all I need to do is take you out of the equation, and then *no one* will ever find it."

Now, he really turns white.

"So, what'll it be, Jorge?" Who chooses a fake name that's just their real name in another language? Even spies and traitors should have higher standards than that.

I let the silence hang, not feeling any need to fill it with more words or threats. My new friend needs time to think, and I'm giving it to him, even though we both know what his answer will be.

He doesn't break the silence, but he nods.

"Good choice," I tell him. Everything is going exactly the way I told Owen and Jessica it would. I can see her sitting at a slot machine behind George but in my line of sight. I wink at her. She ignores me.

Yes, everything is going according to plan. But now comes the part that I didn't share with anyone else.

"Listen, George," I say, forcing him to meet my eyes. "There's one more thing I need you to do."

CHAPTER 20

The Mine

"It's right there," George tells me as I bring Wanderer in close to an asteroid that sits a relatively short flight from the Rishi Paradise. It's a small rock, mined and stripped clean of anything valuable centuries ago, with an ancient and decrepit abandoned mining station as the only evidence humans were ever here. At least on the surface.

Underneath the surface is a different story. The rock is so crisscrossed by mine shafts and tunnels that I suspect a single missile from my old battlecruiser, *Lancer*, would be more than sufficient to break the entire thing up into tiny little dust particles. But, as such things go, the warren of abandoned tunnels makes it an excellent place to hide something you never want to be found by accident.

I might have to revise my original estimate of George Peterson's intelligence.

"Where, exactly?" I ask him from the pilot's chair. He strains to look around the seat in front of him to see the scanner image—there was no way I was going to let him take Lin's co-pilot seat, even if it is vacant right now. He points toward one of the largest and most obvious tunnels, just off the central mining station.

OK, maybe I was starting to give his intelligence too much credit. In a rock full of so many interesting hiding places, he went ahead and picked the most obvious *and* boring of the lot.

George thinks we're alone on *Wanderer*. Lin is currently locked in her cabin. Unfortunately, Owen and his cronies are jammed in there with her as insurance to keep me cooperating. To prevent them from all accidentally meeting George on the six-hour flight from Rishi to this rock, I've kept him in the cockpit with me, except for a few trips to the restroom and one to the galley for some terrible reheated rations.

I bring *Wanderer* close to the abandoned mining station and find a hopeful-looking landing pad that is slightly less crumbled and degraded than the others. Gingerly, I set my new ship down, hoping the ground doesn't collapse underneath it; it shouldn't with the asteroid's feeble gravity, but we're talking about a place that has more in common now with Swiss cheese than a planetoid.

Luckily, *Wanderer* settles into place without

incident, and I put the engines on standby with a lock code only I know. With the talents he and his team have shown so far, I have little doubt Owen can still break the code and make off with my ship if he really wants to, but I'm not going to make things too easy for him. Then, I enter another command into the ship's AI that I hope no one will discover until it's too late.

George and I are already wearing decompression skinsuits from the ship's stores. I now help him affix his helmet and then do my own. We enter the starboard airlock and evacuate the atmo before opening the outer door and climbing down an extendible ladder to the surface of the rock. The gravity is light enough to keep us from floating away, but not much more, so we adopt a weird-looking leaping walk taught to all Navy men and women alike as we head toward the mouth of the target tunnel.

Behind us, I know that Owen and at least one of his goons are following. The agreement—I made a big stink about this before I agreed to contact Jorge and reveal my true identity so that he would lead me to the intel—is for Lin to stay behind on the *Wanderer*, but not before Owen resets her explosive implant. If it takes us more than an hour to get George's package and get back, we have other problems.

"It's about fifty meters in," the traitor tells me morosely through our helmet comms. He's become increasingly sullen the closer we've gotten to our prize. I think it's finally dawned on him that he won't be making the huge payday he was hoping for on this. All I've offered him is his life, but I've also been noticeably vague on how I plan to protect him from the Koratans. Because, truthfully, I don't care what happens to him; I'm only doing this to save Jessica.

"You first," I tell him, just in case he was smart enough to leave any booby traps behind when he hid the thing.

But alas, he wasn't that smart. It takes us about five minutes to get from *Wanderer's* airlock to a modest rockfall inside the tunnel where he's buried a small metal case. He opens it in front of me and shows me a portable memory drive inside, about the size of my finger. I ping it with my implant, using the code I also forced out of him, and I'm now looking at exactly what was so valuable that someone hired Owen to hijack me, my ship, and my first mate.

It's what I expected it to be, which isn't good at all. In fact, it's very, very bad. Because this information is definitely worth killing for, hundreds of times over even, depending on your personal moral code. But I've known choir boys who would probably kill a few dozen people for this particular tidbit. It's worth that much.

Which means, simply, that there is no scenario

where Owen lets me and Jessica out of this alive. Or George, but again, I don't care all that much about the life of a traitor, even if I'm also technically on the run from the same government.

"So, this means I get to live, right?" George asks hopefully.

I glare at him through the helmet. Then, another voice intrudes on our comm channel. "Unfortunately, this is the end for both of you."

Owen.

George's eyes go wide, and he starts blubbering and crying in the helmet. He has no idea who Owen is, but he's already begging him for his life. Some of the promises he makes through the whining are pretty inventive, but it's all to no avail. I know it, and I suspect, deep down, even an imbecile like George knows it.

His annoying pleading stops as Owen cuts him out of the comm channel. "OK, Mendoza," he says to me. "Time to hand it over. You're a dead man, but we might be able to let Commander Lin live if you don't piss me off in the next few minutes."

I turn to regard the man. He and Tucker are both there, emerging from a slight bend in the mine shaft behind us. Tucker's hands are empty, but Owen is holding a pistol aimed squarely at my stomach.

"Hand over the drive," Owen says to me again.

So, I toss it to him. But as it's in the air, I drop a verbal bomb. "It's blank, Owen. I erased it."

I'm gratified to see just from his body language how enraged he is at the thought of coming all this way for nothing, though he does catch the drive and put it in his pocket. Before he can call back to the ship to have Jules kill Jessica, or worse, I speak again. "I copied it first. It's in my implant, behind military-grade encryption. If you want it, you'll need me and Jessica alive and willing."

George picks that moment to start running away, deeper into the mine. For an instant, Owen shifts the gun to aim at the fleeing man but then shifts it back to me, even holding out a hand to stop Tucker from pursuing the man. Without a ship to get him off this rock, the hapless traitor won't be going far.

The mercenary—because I figured out a while back that that's what Owen really is, though not the cool kind like Billy Firebrand, more the evil psychotic kind that always works for the bad guys—turns his eyes back on me through the helmet, and shrugs laconically. "No matter, we'll just kill you later, *after* we kill Miss Lin in front of you. So much for letting her live. Tucker will be disappointed."

I bite back my first response. I can almost *feel* Tucker's anger from the way he tenses next to Owen, but he makes no complaint. The muscle rarely does in outfits like this.

"Maybe," I say carefully, trying to keep my voice as equally unconcerned as Owen's. "Maybe not. You kill her, you'll never get what's in my implant. I'll delete it, and you'll lose. Good luck explaining *that* to your employer."

Owen laughs, which seems a truly inappropriate response at a time like this. But he *is* a psychopath, so inappropriate emotional responses are kind of his thing.

"Really, Brad? How about this? Turn the information over now, and Jessica dies quickly. Don't, and I let Tucker have his way with her first."

I can almost feel the big thug's anger turn into a stupid grin at his boss' words.

I shake my head. "No. This is how it's going to work, Owen. You're going to let me and Jessica go. And then I'll transmit the info to you. Surely, it's worth our lives, especially given what I expect will happen to *you* if you fail to deliver."

Judging by the man's hesitation before he responds, I've finally struck a nerve. But not enough of one because I can see him shake his head in his helmet. "Sorry, Mendoza. Not buying it. I'm thinking that you'll do just about anything to save your pretty little friend from what Tucker has in store for her. Especially if the rumors out of Gerson are true. So, here's my final offer. We all go back to the ship. You transfer the data to me there, then watch your girlfriend die quickly.

Or you can watch Tucker teach her a lesson and *then* give me the data and see her die slowly. Your choice." The jerk isn't even meeting me halfway; some negotiator.

I take a step forward, slumping my shoulders as if in surrender. Owen follows my movements with the gun but otherwise holds his ground. I move to within a couple meters of him and Tucker, and now I can see their facial expressions clearly through their dimly lit helmets. Owen looks bored on the surface, as always, but I can see wariness in his eyes, and one of them is twitching slightly. Even he's feeling the pressure right now at the end. Tucker is more emotive, of course, and if his gaze could kill, I'd be dead a hundred times over. I wink at him just to upset him more.

Now I'm also close enough to see precisely what kind of gun Owen has pointed at my stomach. And suddenly, I have a sliver of hope. It's only a sliver, but I've bet on worse.

I stop moving and widen my stance on the mine shaft floor, with my right foot planted behind me relative to the two men. "I'm not going with you, Owen. So, shoot me now and lose the information, or send Jess out to join me *without* her explosive implant, and I'll let you take my ship and go with the information. Your choice, but I'm done negotiating with a psycho like you."

"Pity," he says without any such emotion in his

voice. "But there's more than one way to get you back to the ship." He points his gun at my left thigh and pulls the trigger.

CHAPTER 21

Tucker Must Die

Nothing happens. Owen pulls the trigger again and again, but nothing. Confused, he looks down at the pistol. That's when I act. In the Billy Firebrand novels, this is where the hero, me, would say something pithy about why the gun won't work and about how non-spacers should never go up against a real spacer like me in a low-grav vacuum.

But witty banter with the bad guy doesn't work in real life. It eliminates the element of surprise, no matter how satisfying it might be to point out the man's mistakes. So, instead of talking, I crouch down, bending my right leg so that I'm kneeling on it for maximum leverage, and I pick up a large rock—discarded mine waste—that's on the ground next to me and which is the reason why I chose to stop in this exact spot.

Before either of the other men can react, I pull the

rock—about the size of a volleyball—to my chest and, with both hands, *push* forward as hard as I can, my low stance and the leg behind me keeping me from flying backward with the effort. Instead, the rock propels out of my hands and straight at Owen's transparent helmet.

Wanderer is a great little ship, but she's not a naval warship. And that means the vac helmets in the ship's stores are simple transparent plastic, not as reinforced and indestructible as what I used in the Navy. So, when the rock hits Owen's helmet, even though it's not moving terribly fast, it's got enough mass and momentum to crack the bubble around his head.

Oh, it's probably not a big enough crack to actually go all the way through the material and let his air escape, but he doesn't know that. He yelps in surprise as the rock hits him, its mass knocking him backward into a slow-motion fall to his butt. His hands fly to his face to cover the crack now right in front of his eyes, which must loom as large for him as a broken battleship spine. In the process, the worthless gun flies from his hand and begins its own slow-motion tumble toward the tunnel floor a few meters away.

"Tucker, take him out!" Owen cries, sounding terrified, as he gets his feet back under him and turns to begin a clumsy, loping run back toward the mouth of the tunnel and the relative safety of *Wanderer*.

I ignore him, focusing all my attention on the big man who is now dramatically cracking his knuckles through the gloves of his skinsuit. Seriously? I thought that was just a cliché in the movies.

Then Tucker takes a step toward me, and I forget to laugh. He truly is *enormous*. And now he's madder than I've ever seen him. So, he does what most big guys try to do at the beginning of a fight. After his first step, he lunges forward, both arms outstretched to grab me in a warm hug and crush the life out of me.

I'm still kneeling on the ground where I threw the rock at Owen, and I make no move to get out of Tucker's way. Instead, I lay down flat on the mine shaft floor. And, just as expected, Tucker overestimates the effect of the asteroid's light gravity and sails right over my head.

As a naval officer and not a Marine, I'm not exactly well-trained in hand-to-hand combat. But I *did* train extensively in low-and-zero g maneuvering. So, while Tucker would surely beat the life out of me in seconds in full gravity, here he's playing on my turf.

It also helps that most of my zero-g training in the Academy was in the form of being my dorm's team captain for slug ball. Think basketball, but with medicine balls in zero-g chambers, where the goal is to use the balls to hit the other team and knock them out of the playing area. It's a brutal game but an Academy favorite, with the instructors just as often betting on the outcome versus trying to dissuade a bunch of competitive eighteen and nineteen-year-olds from hurting each other. It usually resulted in a lot of cracked ribs, but it taught us all about how Newton's third law acts in low-g environments.

And while I don't have any medicine balls nearby now, there are a *lot* of rocks, just like the one I hurled at Owen.

After Tucker sails by overhead, I roll to the side toward another one of the stones I spied earlier. The big man slowly hits the ground behind me, and I can hear his anticipatory grunt through the comm. But it's just a reflex; the gravity isn't enough to even knock the wind out of him.

I make it to my rock and pick it up, rising up on one knee and pivoting to face Tucker, who is ponderously levering himself up and turning to face me.

I throw the rock, again from my chest, just as he launches himself toward me once more, aiming lower this time. That's not great; I was sort of hoping he wouldn't learn from his mistakes that quickly. I guess he does have a brain behind all that meat.

The rock glances off the top of his helmet—I aimed too high, not anticipating his low dive—and I don't have time to move before all of Tucker slams into me, knocking me back and wrenching my knee where I had it planted, as before, on the floor of the mine shaft for leverage.

Now that I'm in the big man's arms, he does just what I expected him to try earlier as we tumble slowly together to the ground: he squeezes…hard.

Full grav or none, it doesn't matter when a guy with arms like an anaconda gets them wrapped around you. I almost instantly lose the breath in my lungs, and any advantage I had over the man is gone.

We bounce once off the ground and then hit again, coming to rest near one of the tunnel walls, my body pinned underneath his. That's when I get supremely lucky. Still working off his normal, full-grav fighting instincts, Tucker momentarily loosens his grip on me and tries to reposition his arms for better effect.

Normally, that would work fine, as he's landed on top of me, and I wouldn't be able to get out from under his bulk fast enough to do anything with that one moment of reprieve. But in low grav…

I push up hard with both hands and bring my knees to my chest, propelling Tucker straight up toward the cavern ceiling. Even in the low grav, he won't fly high enough to hit it—the mine shaft is wide and tall, about five meters both ways—but that's OK because he does fly high enough for me to roll out of the way, so I won't be there when he lands.

A few seconds later, cursing loudly through the comm channel, Tucker hits the mine floor where I used to be and has no time to get his footing before another rock, hurled by yours truly, hits him in the side, sending him sprawling back down in another slow-motion fall before he can even get halfway up. I follow that up with another rock, this time connecting solidly with his helmet, just as I did earlier with Owen.

Like Owen, Tucker gets only a cracked helmet for my trouble, and he's not losing his atmo yet. But the momentum of the stone knocks him over again while I leap up into the air as high as I can go above him and to the right, toward the nearest mine shaft wall. Spinning in the air, I absorb the impact on the wall by bending my knees and then straighten my legs with a hard push, aiming back and down toward the still-prone Tucker, who is on his back and just starting to sit up again.

In my hands is one final rock, which I picked up just before my flying leap, held above my head. Just as I come close to Tucker's helmeted head, I violently slam it down. But I don't let go, adding the momentum and mass of my body to that of the large stone.

The result is exactly what I hoped for. I hear a loud crack through the comm and then another wetter one. The angle of the impact sends me in a sort of tumbling somersault over Tucker, and it takes me a moment to get my feet under me and make my way back over to finish the man off.

I needn't have bothered. Tucker's helmet is shattered, and so is his face. He's not dead yet, but he will be shortly as he tries to take deep, gasping breaths of nonexistent air through his crushed nose and open mouth. It's too late to save him, even if I wanted to.

I stand over him and watch him die. As a mass murderer who once killed 504 civilians, including women and children, and as an ex-Navy captain who has killed countless pirates and more mundane enemies in battle, this is the first time I've killed with my own two hands. It's also the first time I'm actually in a position to watch my victim die up close and personal.

It sickens me, and I have to swallow hard to push back the rising gore that threatens to erupt into my helmet.

Tucker is strong and takes a full minute, even in the vacuum, to fade completely. I could walk away; I *should* walk away—time is of the essence now. But I can't. Tucker is a pig and a bully and probably worse, but it somehow still feels wrong to make him die alone. Or maybe it's more that I feel the need to at least observe the consequences of my actions. Even for a man like me, killing should never be easy. Either way, I wait with him while he lives his last moments.

When the light and hatred finally fade from his eyes, and his gasping attempts at breath stop, I silently turn away, spend another minute or so searching the tunnel floor for one thing I need, and then start a loping run toward the tunnel entrance and *Wanderer*.

CHAPTER 22

Owen's Folly

I find Owen right where I expected, outside my ship, standing clumsily at the top of the ladder to the outer airlock hatch and banging ineffectually on it with one fist. No one answers his frantic knocks, which I take as a good sign or, at the very least, not a bad one.

He can't hear me approach, but some sixth sense seems to warn him, and he turns and leaps down from the top of the ladder, landing lightly on the ground to face me, bouncing once as he fails to properly absorb the landing with his knees the first time.

"Hi, Owen," I say in a weird, almost friendly greeting. I'm a little off-balance, having just completed my first up-close kill, so I think I can be pardoned for not fully embracing the social rules of a situation like this one.

"You locked the ship," he says unnecessarily, so

maybe I'm not the only one unsure of how to approach this new standoff.

I nod through the helmet. "Time lock programmed into the AI. It engaged right after you and Tucker left the ship, and only my code can open the airlocks any time in the next six hours. No one in or out without my say-so."

He nods back, though whether it's in acknowledgment of my statement or admiration for my forethought, I can't tell. Doesn't matter anyway.

"And what's to stop me from calling Jules inside and telling her to go ahead and kill Jessica Lin? Or simply waiting fifteen more minutes until her implant kills her without my signal?"

I shrug. "If you could have called Jules, you would have already done it." It's a good sign that he hasn't been able to reach her yet, though I'm not sure exactly what it means. "Besides, it's all game theory. You had to hurt Jessica before to show me you're serious, but the second you kill her, you lose all leverage over me. And I'm the only one with the intel you desperately want. At this point, it comes down to which one of us flinches first."

He nods, and I can see the hint of a smile through the local star's reflected glare on his helmet. "You truly aren't the idiot people make you out to be, are you?"

"No. I am. But you know what they say about

resourceful idiots..."

He cocks his head quizzically inside the cracked dome.

I step forward, closing the distance between us, and jam the pistol I collected from the mine's floor —where Owen dropped it—right into the man's gut, grabbing his shoulder with my other arm for leverage.

"...there is nothing more dangerous."

I pull the trigger. And, unlike when Owen tried to use it on me, this time, the gun works flawlessly. I feel the buck of the pistol in my hand and see a cloud of red explode from behind his back, the mess of blood and other matter falling slowly to the asteroid's surface. It's disgusting and bile rises again in my throat, so I turn my attention back to him.

With my helmet right up near his, I can see his eyes go wide in pain and disbelief. And I just can't help myself. I'm not sure if it's the fact that this is only my second face-to-face kill or if I've read way too many Billy Firebrand novels. Or maybe it's because I think even a piece of scum like Owen deserves an explanation. Whatever my reasons, I monologue.

"You made a lot of mistakes on this one, Owen. First, you let on far too early that you knew who Jessica and I are. That gave me time to think about how you'd learned what the rest of the galaxy doesn't know.

"Second, you simply didn't grasp the magnitude of what you've gotten involved in. I do. After all, this particular mess is a big part of what killed me the first time around.

"But third," I shut off the comm and press my helmet to his so that he'll still hear me, but no one else can listen in. "You threatened the woman I love. And the second you did that, the only outcome of this was for one of us to die."

Then I take a step back and switch the comm back on. "Finally, you didn't do your research, or you would know that the X-421 Stinger," I raise the pistol for him to see, "has an extra safety for low-g use. It's to prevent an accidental discharge that could send someone tumbling through space if they don't know what they're doing."

I'm still close enough to see the moment Owen dies. And whatever strange sympathy I felt watching Tucker's life leave him eludes me now because I have zero doubt that the galaxy is now a much better place without Owen Thompson in it.

I search his pockets quickly and find a small transmitter with a single button. Its screen shows a countdown with six minutes and fourteen seconds left. Saying a silent prayer, I press the button, and the timer resets to an hour. I breathe a sigh of relief and slump to the asteroid's surface in exhaustion.

CHAPTER 23

The King's Cross...Again

I'm torn now between an overwhelming desire to sleep and an equally strong urge to climb quickly up the ladder, get inside the ship, and make sure Jessica is OK in there with Jules and Harris. I don't even dare call her in case Owen and his team hacked our implant comms.

I start getting up but stop myself from climbing to the airlock. There's one more thing that needs to be done first.

"You shouldn't have hired him," I say softly into my helmet comm.

A figure steps out from behind one of *Wanderer's* landing struts and walks slowly toward me.

"No choice," a woman's voice says without a hint of apology. It's a voice I last heard eight days ago in the Gerson system, threatening to kill me and Jessica if she ever saw us after that. Now, it's oddly comforting to hear it again.

"There's always a choice," I tell Heather Kilgore, Agent of the King's Cross, as she stops a meter from me. Her gun is aimed at my chest, though I've made no effort to point Owen's old gun in her direction.

She shrugs, the move making her military-grade helmet bob up and down a bit. "You're right, of course, but that doesn't change the fact that this was the best way. I needed the traitor and his intel before the Koratans got it, but I needed plausible deniability for the King in case the entire thing blew up; there's no way we can be caught operating in the Leeward Republic. You and Lieutenant Commander Lin were…convenient."

"And Owen?"

She shrugs again. "A mercenary I've used in the past. Willing to do whatever it takes, and usually very effective."

"Well, your plan failed," I tell her simply.

"Did it? I still kept the intel out of the Koratans' hands. And one more dead mercenary isn't—"

"Two," I interrupt her. "Two…dead mercenaries."

She cocks her head and searches my face for a long moment through our respective helmets, then she nods once but says nothing.

"What happens now?" I ask.

"Well, that depends on you. But tell me first, how did you know to have Petty Officer Peterson contact me?"

That was the last thing I'd told George to do back in the casino restaurant, instructing him to send a specific message to a comm code I'd found deep within *Wanderer's* memory on the first day I'd flown her away from Gerson. It was a gamble, but I suspected the code belonged to the ship's former owner. Turns out, I was right. And having George send the message would keep it a secret even if Owen had found a way to break my implant's encryption. He made the call as soon as we were clear of the casino's jamming.

But I don't tell her all of that. I just tell her the little that matters. "Owen said we were after a traitor from the Layton System Patrol, but there hasn't been anyone AWOL from there in over five years. But there *was* a George Peterson who went missing from Gerson several weeks ago. Idiot thought changing his name to Jorge was enough."

She nods, apparently impressed. "He was on loan to the survey corps ship that actually found the stellarium deposit in Gerson's asteroid belt. Wainwright may have sold the existence of the deposit to the Koratans, but Peterson could have told them its *exact* location."

"And if the exact location got out, the Koratans would send *everything* they've got to take it from Prometheus."

"Yes," she confirms; I'm on a roll here. "You saw

first-hand what the Koratans were willing to do even just knowing there was a deposit *somewhere* in the system. Imagine what they'd do with the exact coordinates. Pure chaos. And if the information got out to other nations…"

I nod again, numb and not particularly caring if good ole King Charles loses the most valuable deposit of metal in the Fringe. "So again," I ask her, "what happens now?"

"Well, if you're asking if I'm going to kill you, I don't think I will. You and Lin proved valuable for a second time in just the last two weeks. And I may need to use you again, so keeping you alive is the best choice. Besides, why punish you for providing yet another valuable service to the Crown?"

I huff. Even after she let us go the first time, the idea of a King's Cross agent with a conscience amuses me. "And what's to stop you from sending the rest of the King's Cross, or the Navy, after us later?"

She smiles just a bit. "Think of it as mutually assured destruction. The King wanted you dead, so you're dead. If he finds out otherwise, he'll hunt you down ruthlessly across the galaxy. But also…"

"He'll know you lied to him," I finish for her.

She nods.

"Of course," I admit, "that still doesn't stop you from killing us yourself. And the whole thing about us being useful, I don't buy it. Because, like you said, having us alive is a threat to your life as well. If *anyone* finds out who we are," I look down meaningfully at Owen's corpse, "whether you tell them or they figure it out for themselves, you'll be as good as dead. So, tell me the real reason I'm not lying next to our friend right now."

There's a long silence, and I think she's going to refuse outright. But then I hear her sigh. "Like we talked about at Gerson, what happened to Jessica Lin on *Persephone* was wrong. And let's just say I have...firsthand experience with just how wrong."

I nod. There's no more explanation needed.

But she continues speaking anyway. "And what happened to her on *Ordney* was almost worse. She deserves better. Call it feminine solidarity if that makes you feel better."

"What happened on *Ordney*?" I ask softly.

She shakes her head. "Not my place to tell you. Only Lin can make that choice."

It's what I expected, but you can't blame a guy for trying.

"Now," she says, "speaking of Miss Lin, perhaps you'd better go and make sure she's OK. But not before you give me what I came here for."

I motion down toward Owen's body. "Right breast pocket."

She keeps her gun pointed in my direction but

crouches and quickly searches the body, finding and pocketing the drive in her own skinsuit. I see her eyes go momentarily out of focus as she accesses it with her implant.

"So, you didn't delete it. You were *bluffing*?" She's apparently been listening in the entire time. Good of her to help me in the fight against the two mercenaries.

I shrug. "There wasn't enough time. But a guy like Owen expects a double-cross, so I gave him one to believe in."

"And the copy you made on your implant?"

"Another bluff. The drive was copy-proof." I give her temporary root access to my implant so she can double-check that I'm telling the truth. Left unsaid is that I could have still memorized the coordinates from it, but she doesn't ask, and I don't tell. "Besides, by now, George Peterson has no doubt gotten himself completely lost in those tunnels, but I'm sure a woman with your ingenuity and resources can find him and make sure no other copies exist."

She doesn't acknowledge my suggestion verbally but starts to walk toward the tunnel mouth, confident enough to leave me at her back with a loaded gun. But I'm done killing for today...well, almost. There are still two of Owen's team on my ship with Jessica, and they'll be getting antsy that their boss isn't back by now."

I start climbing the ladder to the airlock to punch in the code and enter my ship. But before I'm done, I hear Heather Kilgore's voice one more time. "You know, you'd make a halfway decent mercenary yourself. Expect a call from me in the future. I seem to find myself suddenly short of resources in this sector of space."

I don't respond directly, because she and I both know the truth. If she calls, I'll have no choice but to answer. Instead, I say, "I do have two requests before you blast off back to Promethean space." And then I tell her what they are. To my surprise, she agrees to both.

CHAPTER 24

The Real Femme Fatale

I find Jessica in the Wanderer's galley. I have the pistol out and extended in front of me, struggling to remember what I learned nearly a decade ago when I participated in my last boarding action—before I reached too lofty a rank for the Navy to risk me behind a gun like that.

But there's no need. Jessica is standing with her back against the galley counter, a gun in *her* hand pointed squarely at me as I enter the room. She's still wearing the dress from Rishi, and one of the shoulders is ripped, but otherwise, she looks to be in one piece. When she sees it's me and not Owen or Tucker, she lets her shoulders droop as tension flows out of them, and she swings the gun back around to cover the two other people in the galley.

Harris sits calmly at the galley table, his hands flat on the tabletop where Jessica and I can easily see them. Jules, however, is tied to her chair with a gag in her mouth, glaring hatefully in turns at me,

Jessica, *and* Harris.

I clearly missed all the fun, but I'm duly impressed. I almost died taking out just Tucker in an environment where I had a huge advantage. Somehow, Lin managed to subdue and capture two mercenaries seemingly without much trouble, though from the way she stands favoring one side, her broken ribs aren't doing too well. Also, the fact that Harris isn't even tied up indicates she may have had only one that actually fought back. Still, I'm impressed beyond measure.

"You good?" I ask my first mate.

"No," she says, a tremor in her voice. "The hour passed, but someone needs to get this *thing* out of my head." I suddenly feel terrible for not coming into the ship sooner. While I was chatting with Kilgore outside, Jessica must have been a wreck counting down the hour and not knowing I'd already reset the timer.

But maybe I can make up for that. I look over at Harris, and he nods once. So, I take a leap of faith and carefully hand him the transmitter I took off Owen's body. He fiddles with it for a second and then nods again. "It's inert now," he tells us. "You can dig out the implant at any time, but the explosive is no longer armed."

I see Jessica's shoulders drop further, and for a second, I think she might collapse in exhaustion like I almost did on the asteroid's surface. But she keeps her footing, and the gun in her hand never wavers from covering the two mercenaries.

I move over to stand beside her, my pistol now pointed squarely at Jules. Slowly, hesitantly, I reach up and put my other arm around Jessica's shoulders. And then, the floodgates open.

In a Billy Firebrand story, this is the part where the beautiful woman cries into the hero's shoulder. But this isn't a fictional adventure, and it's me now sobbing as I hold tight to Jessica, the pain, stress, frustration, and guilt of the last few days—perhaps even longer—coming out in choking, very unmanly sobs.

She cries a bit, too, and even leans her head into my chest, but I'm the one who ugly cries. And, you know what? It feels amazing.

CHAPTER 25

A New Crew Member

Fifteen minutes later, Jules is sitting on the deck of Wanderer's airlock, still loosely tied up but dressed now in a decompression skinsuit. Next to her are a helmet, a long-range comm, and a few days' supply of extra air bladders. I crouch down in front of her, thankful she's still gagged, so I can't understand the very colorful grunts originating from her.

I pick up the helmet, but before I put it on her head, I lean forward and whisper so only she can hear. "You know, it would have never worked between us. Your butt is pretty nice, but not nearly good enough to make up for your terrible personality."

She glares at me and starts a whole new string of undoubtedly creative invectives rendered ineffective by the gag. I seal the helmet, further muffling her tirade.

Then I turn to regard Harris, who is also wearing a

skinsuit and is about to put his own helmet on. I've reached a decision—an important one. But first, I look over at Jessica, standing outside the airlock, who gives me a nod of permission.

"Harris," I say, "you want a ride somewhere?"

He stops with his helmet halfway on. "Actually, I was hoping to sign on. Be part of..." he looks around as if to encompass us and all of *Wanderer* around us, "whatever this is. I like the way you operate."

I nod. I half expected that response. And given his skills with disguises, he'll be useful to two semi-fugitives on the run. Though we may have to work on his own atrocious appearance. Plus, of all Owen's team, he's ultimately the one I grew to hate the least.

He and I leave the airlock and go back into the ship's corridor, sealing the hatch behind us. Then, I override the controls, blowing open the outer hatch without first evacuating the atmo. I can't help it, and I laugh out loud as a still tied-up Jules is forcibly sucked out through the hatch and falls slowly and comically to the asteroid's surface. Even Jessica can't entirely suppress a snicker.

Of course, Lin wouldn't laugh if she knew what I know, that Jules won't be alive for long. Heather Kilgore will see to that after she finds George Peterson, and I doubt either of them will ever leave this rock. Part of me is sad about that fact, but I also recognize the expediency. They know about me and Jessica, and that's as much a threat to Kilgore as it is to us. Besides, one is a traitor who sold out his country, and the other is a sadistic killer who might chase us forever if she got free.

But I'm glad Jessica doesn't know. Best that only one of us has to live with their deaths on his conscience. I can at least protect her from that.

As I turn to head back to the cockpit to lift the ship off this horrid little rock, Jessica close on my heels, Harris asks, "So, any chance you can tell me what it is we'll be doing? What are we?"

I turn back as Jessica answers first. "We're mercenaries," she says, smiling in my direction.

"Nope," I say quickly, though it pains me to do so. "We're a legitimate cargo ship." I open a file on my implant, the one Heather Kilgore gave me in response to one of my last requests on the asteroid's surface, and I send it to Jessica's implant.

Her eyes widen momentarily when she receives the fully signed-over registration for the *Wanderer*, though under its original name, *Hornet*. She searches my eyes, probably trying to see if I'm serious about being a simple freighter captain from here on out now that we have the proper credentials.

Whether she finds in my eyes what she's looking for or not, I can't say. But she turns away from me and looks back toward Harris. "No," she says in the

Confident Lin voice that sends good chills up and down my spine. "We're mercenaries."

"Wait! I'm Billy Firebrand?" I exclaim unable to hold my tongue or keep the excitement out of my voice. It's been a long day, and my normally modest self-control is pretty much gone at this point. "Like, for real?"

She turns back to regard me with a long-suffering expression. "Sure, Brad. You can be Billy Firebrand, whoever that is."

"And that makes you Nikita Starshine. And Harris is Scooter James. This is going to be awesome!" Apparently I get inappropriately giddy when I'm exhausted and just killed two men.

She sighs loudly and rolls her eyes; then she smiles and says, with laughter in her voice, "Brad, you're an idiot."

Those four words have never sounded better.

CHAPTER 26

To Forgive is Divine

Later, Jessica and I are sitting in *Wanderer's* cockpit as we fly away from the little Swiss cheese asteroid. We lost no time leaving; I want to be well clear of the rock before Heather Kilgore finds George Peterson and Jules and then blasts off from wherever she's hidden her ship. Jessica, who still has no idea Kilgore was ever there, seems equally anxious to leave the place behind.

We sit there in silence for a long time, maybe a full hour. Harris is nowhere to be seen, probably in his new cabin sorting through his feelings at leaving his old life behind. I know what that's like, so I give him his space.

I've settled on and then rejected about a dozen things I want to say to my first mate—a dozen different lame but heartfelt apologies for what I said to her back on Rishi—but she's the one to speak first.

"I'm sorry, Brad."

Wait. What?!

"Uh, Jess. I don't mean to sound rude, but why are *you* apologizing to *me*?"

She looks at me, eyebrows knit in confusion. She still has the lash extensions and the eye shadow from Harris' makeover on Rishi, and they accentuate the effect. "For what I said about your ex-wife back in the casino. I was upset and jumped to some conclusions, and I know I really hurt you."

Now I'm speechless again. Literally. I'm opening my mouth, trying to get words to come out, but the only thing I manage sounds like someone is letting the air slowly out of a balloon. Super manly. Just like Billy Firebrand.

She looks confused again but says nothing as I choke on my words. Finally, I manage to eke out, almost in a whisper, "But…what I said to you. I…I didn't mean to hurt you."

Understanding dawns in those beautiful eyes, and she smiles at me. "Is that why you've been so quiet? I thought it was because of what *I* said to *you*. I mean, what you said about me not knowing what a healthy relationship looks like…well, it hurt, and I was really angry with you for a few hours, but you were right. And even if it wasn't the nicest thing to say…" she shrugs. "Listen, your entire world had just come crashing down around you; I can't blame you if you lashed out in the moment."

"OK," I say in consternation. "But you have to know that I'm sorry, too. And, for what it's worth, I'm pretty sure you were right about Carla." It hurts to say that, but just voicing it out loud somehow also seems to lift a small part of a massive weight from my shoulders.

She looks back at me now, graces me with another of her rare smiles, and reaches out a hand to place on mine like she did back at the bar and grill. It sends an electric charge through my entire body. For a long time, we just sit that way, enjoying the moment.

Lin is again the one who breaks the silence. You couldn't make me do it for all the stellarium in the galaxy.

"So, where do we go from here, Captain?"

I want to take her in my arms, kiss her, and say something smooth about how it doesn't matter where we go as long as we're together. But there are lines that, once crossed, can never be uncrossed. If she doesn't feel the same way, and I'm almost certain she doesn't, things will forever be awkward between us. And right now, I need her with me like I need oxygen to breathe, even if she isn't with me in the way I truly want. And even if it means no more booze...at least around her.

So, I keep it simple. "Well, we're mercenaries now. We look for someone willing to pay us to shoot at things. Should be easy; everyone wants something shot now and again."

She laughs and squeezes my hand, and it's the best I've felt about myself in the six months since Bellerophon.

EPILOGUE

I slam awake, disoriented and wondering where I am and what that infernal high-pitched wailing in my ears could be. Luckily, after so many years of Navy conditioning—not to mention almost a week without a drink—I gather my wits quickly and find myself in Wanderer's pilot seat with the alarm coming from the console in front of me. I check it quickly.

Proximity alert?

I'm alone in the cockpit, and a quick time check reveals it's been nine hours since we burned away from the small asteroid; we're still one hour short of the jump point back to the Kate's Hope system, where we collectively decided to return if for no other reason than to get out of Fiori space as quickly as possible.

I recall now that I sent Lin back to her quarters to sleep a few hours ago, and Harris is likely still resting as well. I must have dozed off because I didn't even notice...

My heart sinks, and I swear loudly as I see what's triggered the proximity alert. The sensor picture resolves at the same time the massive ship moves overhead and becomes visible in the cockpit's forward viewport, reversing thrust to match velocities with my little freighter.

It's a warship. And not just any warship. This is no simple patrol boat, but a full-fledged battlecruiser ten times longer than *Wanderer*. And while I might not immediately recognize its design, I don't need to know what star nation it's from to see the dozens of laser turrets that look like they're aimed right at my head through the cockpit window.

"*Merchant Vessel Wanderer*," a professionally cool female voice sounds from the comm, "this is the *Leeward Republic Navy Ship Dauntless*. This is a system patrol stop. Heave to and prepare to be boarded."

I immediately cut acceleration and send a quick acknowledgment. *Wanderer* can't outrun a battlecruiser, and all it would take is a twitch on the controls of one of those laser turrets to vaporize my ship and its small crew. I want the captain of that behemoth to be one hundred percent assured I'm not going to make a run for it.

"Jennifer! Harris!" I shout through the internal comm, using Jessica's false name in the event the *Dauntless* is already hacked into our shipboard transmissions. "We've got company! Meet me at the..." I check the sensor picture "...starboard airlock."

The ship shudders around me as the battlecruiser grasps us in a docking clamp. I unstrap from the pilot's seat and head out the cockpit door toward the airlock, making haste. My hand automatically goes to my belt where I've been carrying Owen's pistol, but it's not there, left behind in the cockpit. No matter; a simple handgun wouldn't be of any use against a ship full of trained spacers and Marines. Even having it might actually get me shot before I can figure out what they want.

I arrive at the airlock before either Jessica or Harris, which is fine. Better for me to face this first as the captain. That gives me pause; I'm not sure when I started thinking of myself unironically as the captain again. But old habits of command are once again kicking in, though they come with a sober lack of confidence that I'll be able to get us out of whatever this is.

I have no idea why a Leeward Republic Navy vessel would not only sneak up on *Wanderer* but then demand to board us with no preamble, but it can't be good. And it would be far too much of a coincidence for this *not* to be related to what happened just half a day ago on that lonely asteroid, which makes it doubly not good for us.

Further speculation on my part is cut off when the outer airlock hatch opens without protest, the boarding party entering a manufacturer's override code that my ship's AI has no choice but to accept. Not wanting to appear like we have anything to hide, I check the pressure and then key open the inner airlock hatch to save them the trouble.

Only to find myself staring down the business ends of four light assault rifles pointed straight at my face.

I automatically raise my hands. "Uh, hi," I say through a suddenly dry mouth, "can I help you?"

With an effort, I look beyond the looming rifles to see a bemused look on one of the Marines' faces at my question. There are three men and one woman, all dressed in identical uniforms that are foreign to me, but they are still instantly identifiable as Marines in their stance and the steady hold on their rifles. That and they each look like they could break me in half without a second thought.

"Are you the captain of this vessel?" asks the same stern female voice that ordered me to prepare to be boarded over the comm. Looking past the Marines, I now see an older woman in what looks more like a naval uniform. From the marks on her collar, I think she might be a rear admiral of all things. Now this *really* isn't looking good for us.

"Uh, yeah?" I respond to her. I didn't mean for it

to sound like a question, but given I just woke up from a nap after fighting for my life for two days straight, I'm willing to forgive myself. You might think that after conducting so many routine boarding operations in my time in the Navy, I would know what to do here, but I've never been on *this* side of those guns. Besides, you don't send battlecruisers, battle-ready Marines, and a rear admiral for a routine inspection stop.

"Good," she says with a curt nod. "Where is the rest of your crew?"

I shrug without lowering my hands. "Coming, I think. We were all asleep."

She frowns as if I've just committed some cardinal sin by being asleep at the wheel of a starship, which maybe I have. I'm unfamiliar with the navigation laws in the Leeward Republic, but either way, I don't think she's the type to let me off with a warning.

Before I can open my mouth and ask the stern woman what's going on, an older man in an expensive-looking civilian business suit steps up beside her. He's reasonably tall, about my height, and Asian, with perfectly combed black hair that's graying at the temples, the only feature that betrays his age. His face looks even more dour than the naval officer next to him, giving the impression of a man who only smiles for corporate

PR photos. He gives me a quick once over before looking past me into my ship. Then he speaks.

I can't understand anything he says; it's in what sounds like Mandarin to my untrained ear, but I could be wrong. I'm about to tell them so when I hear a familiar female voice answer in the same language from behind me.

Without lowering my hands, I turn my head to see Jessica stepping up next to me, staring at the older man, a grim set to her mouth.

"Uh…Jen?" I ask.

Lin shakes her head but keeps her hard stare on the man with the graying temples, matching his glare for its intensity. "It's OK, Brad, they know who we are. No use hiding it." Then she sighs loudly.

"Hello, father."

THE END

If you enjoyed this book, please leave a review!

There are more adventures to come for
Brad Mendoza and Jessica Lin.

BOOKS BY THIS AUTHOR

The Worst Ship In The Fleet (Book One Of Dumb Luck And Dead Heroes)

Brad Mendoza is an idiot. He knows it, and so does everyone else. A promising naval career down the drain just because he accidentally killed 504 civilians. So, it's time for him to give up and accept a dead-end command on Persephone, the worst ship in the fleet. Until he meets the beautiful and cunning Jessica Lin, his new executive officer who harbors a terrible secret of her own. Now, he's in a race to save her and his stupid ship.

But Brad Mendoza is an idiot. We'll just have to hope that he's the lucky kind.

The Truth (Book One Of The Four Worlds Saga)

Pursued by a relentless assassin, Alan and Jinny race across the galaxy in search of a secret truth that has eluded humanity for centuries.

The Four Worlds: The Truth is the epic first volume of an imaginative and immersive Science Fiction series, equally suitable for adults and YA, that will take you on a fast-paced thrill ride across the galaxy. From lush jungle planets to planet-spanning metropolises and everything in between, the universe of the Four Worlds shows humanity at its best and worst. Buckle up for this unforgettable saga of government deception, unexpected heroes, and the indomitable human spirit!

I enjoyed this saga immensely...an excellent debut novel and an exciting series opener. I highly recommend it to fans of space opera, and military and genetic engineering sci-fi buffs..."
-Sheri Hoyte, Reader Views

Subversion (Book Two Of The Four Worlds Saga)

Earth has been warned! But when the Council Navy shows up on their doorstep, they are woefully unprepared.

The Four Worlds: Subversion is the second volume of an imaginative and immersive adult and YA Science Fiction series that will take you on a fast-paced thrill ride across the galaxy.

Space battles, intergalactic pursuits, heists, prison breaks, and profound plot twists await you in this unforgettable saga of governmental deception and unexpected heroes.

"...a highly exciting and mind-bending text that presents well-scripted themes of perfidy, susceptibility, and risk...highly recommended for young minds who love space operas and adventures, as well as futuristic worlds."
-Ephantus M., Reader Views

ABOUT THE AUTHOR

Skyler Ramirez

Mr. Ramirez writes science fiction and fantasy that entertains, thrills, uplifts, and inspires. His books contain surprising plot twists that keep you guessing, exciting universes that fuel the imagination, and thought-provoking drama that keeps you coming back for more. But at the end of the day, all of his writing centers around one theme: how relatively ordinary men and women can do extraordinary things. As a student of history, he believes this to be true and loves exploring the motivations and deeply held beliefs and dreams of his characters.

Skyler writes books that adults will enjoy but that he wouldn't be embarrassed or worried for his teenage children to read. He feels that great stories don't need foul language, graphic scenes, or other window dressing to make them exciting. A good story stands on its own.

Mr. Ramirez lives with his wife, Lindsey, and their four children in Texas. When he is not writing, he has been and continues to be a leader and executive with multiple Fortune 500 and Fortune 1000 companies.

He would love it if you subscribed to his newsletter, which you can do at https://www.skylerramirez.com.